A Token OF MY Affliction

For Mark & Lyn

from

Love

A Token of My Affliction

Janette Platana

Tightrope Books Inc.
2 College Street, Unit 206-207
Toronto, ON M5G 1K3
www.tightropebooks.com

Editor: Deanna Janovski
Typography: Dawn Kresan
Cover design: Lauren Barless
Author photo credit: Esther Vincent

We thank the Canada Council for the Arts and the Ontario Arts
Council for their support of our publishing program. Printed
and bound in Canada.

Library and Archives Canada Cataloguing in Publication

Platana, Janette, author
    A token of my affliction / Janette Platana.

Short stories.
    ISBN 978-1-926639-75-8 (PBK.)
    I. TITLE.

PS8631.L399T63 2014   C813'.6   C2014-903020-7

This book is dedicated to bpNichol

Bloodline

She comes upon the clearing and a word arrives with the bird: *ballgown*. It pops into her head just like that, maybe because the bird, a cardinal, reminds her of a woman in a red, fancy dress. But no, a red bird like that is most certainly a male bird, and a male would not wear a ballgown. Not that a bird would wear a dress at all, of course, so it is maybe doubly or even triply stupid of her to hear the word *ballgown* in her head when she sees a bird in the woods. But the word flew into her head like the bird flew into the clearing, and the word and the bird landed at the same moment.

Gail stands in the clearing. The cardinal stands in the clearing. The bird stares back at her, still, still, still. Gail feels a sudden sharp tug, as if the bird were about to swallow her into its eye. She shakes her head sharply, and the bird flies up into the high branches of a cedar.

So now she is alone. By rights, Gail should have found her daughter Sophie here, not the red bird. Gail is here looking for Sophie, who has run ahead of her into these woods. It's an almost game, an almost agreement: if Sophie is upset, she "runs away" and Gail follows her and "finds" her in the clearing, where Sophie waits. The woods are technically part of the city's wildish ravine, but the hill that is their backyard runs straight down into the woods, and they've never put up a fence.

Today, Sophie has "run away" because some girls at school have uninvited her to a birthday party. Sophie has "trouble with friends." That's how the teacher broke it to Gail. Sophie makes friends quickly, but then something goes wrong. She quarrels with the other girls, surprising them with her hostility. She is violent in her play, though not toward her classmates. Still, it seems to scare them, and Sophie is often the target of some small girl-on-girl campaign. Gail and the teacher agree, not for the first time, that Sophie is struggling. She is bright in classwork, and maybe even talented in art class, but she has trouble. Gail promises again that she will find a way or a person to help Sophie with her—her what, exactly? Her temper? Her grief? Sophie is nine.

So Gail had broached the topic of "getting along" with Sophie carefully. "I know about it, you stupid stupid," Sophie had cried and rounded on Gail with a long-armed punch. Gail turned to miss the blow, and Sophie's fist caught her on the breast. Her little face furious, sweaty and pinched. "I know everything!" Then a runaway bolt for the woods and the clearing.

Sophie began running away when Gail was diagnosed four years ago. She ran away regularly during Gail's chemo and radiation. Once, when Sophie had run away and Gail had followed her, Sophie insisted Gail lie down on her back in the grass. Gail obliged; she was tired and ill from her second treatment, and the jog along the path to the clearing had made her head throb. Sophie made Gail lie down on the grass and placed a firm piece of moss the size of her five-year-old hand on Gail's forehead.

"Look at the sky until it spins," Sophie ordered. "When it starts to spin, your wings'll get really big and dig into the ground. That way, you stick on. Careful. It hurts." Gail looked over at Sophie out of the corner of her eye, careful not to move her head and disturb the moss. Sophie was grimacing, her mouth pulled open into a bared-teeth frown, and her eyes were held wide open. She was staring into the sun and crying open eyed.

Now Gail stands alone in the clearing and rubs the spot where Sophie's punch landed. For the third or fourth time this month she feels and doesn't feel a small lump there, on the underside of the right breast. She feels it and then she doesn't feel it. She must be wrong. It's about the size of a pebble: bigger than a pea, smaller than an acorn. She doesn't call Sophie, knows she must be nearby and knows that Sophie won't answer her even if she does call. She's not scared yet.

Gail turns her face up to the too blue, too bright sky. She can hear the cardinal in the cedars, his song like a fast, cold creek over a rocky bottom. Gail tilts her head back so her neck hurts and stares at the sky until she can feel the earth spinning. And then she lies down.

She's lying down in the clearing, on her back, and she can feel the earth spin. She senses rather than hears Sophie in the woods, at the edge of the clearing.

"You're sick again, aren't you?" Sophie lies down on the grass beside her mother.

Gail wonders how she knows. Sophie presses her head against Gail's right breast, and her head, or the breast, is so hot that Gail wonders if one of them is feverish. She puts her arm tight around Sophie. She should speak, should say something to her daughter. Her tongue has thickened in her mouth, and when she swallows it feels like a dull blade in her throat.

"Sophie." She gets that far. She gets that far and Sophie says, "I can make you better again. I'll make you better, like I did last time."

For the last four years, Gail has held her love for her daughter at arm's length from her heart. The heart breaks open in love. Gail has known this and avoided this, this breaking open, this gaping, this wide-eyed weeping.

For a minute, Gail expects Sophie to get up and search for a patch of moss, but Sophie lies still next to her mother. The two of them stare up at the circle of sky. The cardinal slices across the circle of blue, intersecting it, bloodline incision across a blind eye.

"Ballgown," Sophie says.

Renee is Bewildered

Renee is bewildered by infancy.

Not just bewildered in the way that all mothers are by their new-born babies (although she is in that way, too), Renee is freaked out in an additional way, because it is different, this baby, her baby: it talks.

And nothing could have prepared her for the teeth.

When the baby slithered out of her and into the delivery doctor's gloved hands, he saw the teeth and, passing the squiggle to a nurse, muttered, "neonatal dentate." The nurse swished a finger back and forth inside the baby's mouth, looking for a cleft palate. None. In fact, the baby had so far scored negative for Ellis-van Creveld and pachyonychia congenita. Renee enjoys hearing the names of all the syndromes her baby doesn't have; she is very tired, and the susurration of the syllables is soothing as ocean waves.

In the private room her mother has paid for, Renee is brought a post-delivery meal of tea and beef broth. After labouring for twelve hours, Renee wants a cheeseburger with a side of pasta and a chocolate bar, and as she drinks her dinner, she decides that as soon as the baby falls asleep, she will call her favourite restaurant and ask them to deliver.

The first latch, the first nurse, no problem. The teeth cause her no discomfort at all, thank goodness. The baby drains her breast efficiently with what must be a minus-three PSI suction.

And this is when the baby speaks his first words: "Merci, ma chère." Because of his mouthful of teeth—twenty, Renee had counted—his pronunciation is exquisite.

She is too astonished to respond, so as the baby drops into milk-drunk sleep, she is left to worry that her French is not very good.

The restaurant delivery arrives: a take-out container full of fettuccine in white sauce and an airline-sized bottle of the restaurant's house red. As Renee eats, she rakes her mind for remnants of grade-eight core French and practises a few phrases under her breath. When the baby's eyes flutter open she says to him, "Bon matin."

"Tengo hambre, por favor," he replies and opens his little mouth wide, showing white molars. "La leche," he prompts, his head tilted back.

He has a little voice, as you would expect a baby might.

He does not speak at all in front of the nurse who comes in to weigh him, although he does slide his glance meaningfully over to Renee. Then he gives her a broad, stagey wink. Holding her astonished gaze, he smiles, showing his teeth. In that moment, Renee discovers the involuntary smile of motherhood, the one where the mouthcorners of mother and baby seem controlled by the same heartstrings; when the corners of the baby's mouth go up, so do hers, instantly, automatically, even though she is thinking, *What the??*

The nurses have been pretty matter-of-fact about the neonatal dentata. The newborn mouth full of teeth. They must see a lot worse, Renee reflects, watching the nurse leave the room on soft soles.

"Ciao," says Freddie to the nurse's retreating back.

So far, French and Spanish. Now Italian. What's next? Greek? Latin? Aramaic?

Renee gives in to sleep—or rather, sleep gives itself to her—lulled by words she does not entirely understand.

When Renee wakes, her mother is there, sitting in a chair against the wall, waiting. Her hair is perfectly arranged, dyed an absolutely convincing and youthful ash blond. Her suede boots match the suede trim of her short leather jacket, and the jeans and silk sweater she wears are the earthy, casual elegant that only a great deal of money can manage.

Feeling her daughter's eyes on her, Renee's mother glances up from the magazine she is reading, glances down again to finish the paragraph, then puts it aside.

With a sigh, she crosses to Renee's bedside, pats her daughter's hand, and says, "Well, that's over with. What's the baby's name?"

"Alfredo," says Renee without thinking.

"We're not Italian, Renee," says her mother.

Renee says nothing. She wants to retort, "We're not French, either," but doesn't. She has gone through life not correcting people when she is called Reenee, Renny, or Rainy.

Her mother sighs again, as though Renee has spoken aloud.

"We can call him Freddie, I suppose," her mother continues, pulling on a pair of gloves that match the boots. "I'll have the car come for you in the morning."

As an afterthought, turning at the doorway, she adds, "Congratulations."

"Thank you," answers Renee.

"She's a piece of work," offers Freddie, squashed low and neckless in a swaddling of blankets tucked into Renee's elbow.

She is about to reply when Freddie says, "Goody! Someone's coming!"

This last bit is because someone, the doctor from the delivery room, is entering, carrying a clipboard, leading a phalanx of white-coated hospital staff.

"Mrs. Uh … " says the doctor, to his chart.

"Renee," Renee says.

"Thank you, Mrs. Renee. As you may have learned, neonatal teeth are quite rare, and some of the interns are interested in the opportunity to view this phenomenon. Do you mind?"

"Not at all," replies Freddie, opening wide.

Everyone in the room looks startled, except the baby, whose eyes are closed, head tipped up and back.

"Not at all. Not at all," says Renee, covering for him, pitching her voice differently each time, trying to get it to sound smaller and higher like Freddie's. "I mean, go right ahead. Look! He even has his mouth open for some reason. Isn't that odd?"

Then she says, as if the doctor or one of the interns had replied, "Not at all. Not at all. Not at all," a few more times, feeling like a ventriloquist's dummy. She wants to say, "Dottle of deer! Dottle of deer!" with her own teeth clenched in a smile, to prove something, but she's not sure what, so she just keeps the smile twitching on her face and waits.

The doc, a dumb-looking guy with great big hands—ugh, Renee suddenly remembers them scrabbling around inside her birth canal—approaches Freddie, who has brought his lips together in a wet, pretty smirk. Bedside, the doctor says in a surprisingly soft tone, "Think we can get him to open up?" petting the baby's soft cheek with one giant fingertip.

Nothing doing. Doctor Big Mitts frowns. Inside the blanket, Renee pinches Freddie lightly. He lets out a howl, uppers and lowers on brief but impressive display, then slams them shut, his eyes roving the room. He glares at them all then pulls his lips tight as the opening of a drawstring purse.

The doctor is still trying to appear unruffled before his students.

"Ha, ha," he laughs.

"Open up, please, Freddie," says Renee sweetly.

Freddie opens a little, makes a little hole between his lips the size of a corn niblet.

"It's almost as if he understands," says one of the interns.

"Maybe if you encourage him to nurse," says Dr. Bigmitts. "Offer him the breast."

The little opening is still there. Renee "offers him the breast." She holds it out to him. It's the size of his head. She pokes his mouth opening with the nipple. It's like trying to pick a lock with a brick.

Nothing doing. The doctor is herding the white coats out. Renee drags her nipple across the baby's compressed frown.

"Wait!" cries Renee. Freddie has latched on. The doctors have gone.

The baby looks up at her resentfully.

"What?" says Renee. He's not nursing, just glowering, latched on like a trout. Renee breaks the latch with her finger.

"What did you do that for?" the baby gripes.

"Can't you cooperate?" she asks.

"Come on, let's nurse," he says, smacking his lips open. "Come on, I'm a baby. Nurse me up."

Renee hesitates.

"Come on," he says. "It's nurse-on-demand. I'm demanding."

She offers.

"Obrigado, minha mãe," he says and gets to it.

After only a few long gulps, his eyes roll gently up toward sleep, then back down to lock with hers, still only partly awake.

Aloud, she wonders, "Where did you come from? Do you know?"

The baby doesn't answer. His long, long lashes are settling onto his cheek, wing tips brushing a snowdrift.

The heavy lids close.

He sleeps.

She sleeps.

He wakes.

"Come on, baby," he says, in English. "You know what I want." Opening his lips wide.

"Freddie," she says, thrusting the nipple in, "you must have an Oedipus complex."

"Au contraire, my dear," he responds, turning his face up to hers. "If the Greek gods had had a motto, it would have been Fuck Everybody, not just Fuck Your Mother. The way the Greek gods went at it, they would have given Oedipus full marks for coupling with Iocaste. The truth of *Oedipus Rex* is You Cannot Avoid Your Destiny."

He just stares back at her while she stares at him.

Finally, she bursts, "Freddie! You're a baby!"

"I need hardly repeat what he said concerning young children dying almost as soon as they were born. Of piety and impiety to gods and parents, and of murderers, there were retributions other and greater far which he described."

He pauses. Then adds, "*The Republic*. Book X. The Myth of Er. Do you know it?"

Renee finds that she does know it, knows that in it, a genius chooses a pre-existent soul to be the guardian of its life and the fulfiller of its choices. She knows this as knowledge remembered, not taught. She got the classics prize in her senior year. She thinks about Plato for a while and the Myth of Er and the business about the word genius and what it's come to mean. The Greek for it is *daemon*, but the Romans translated it and now *daemon* means *devil*, and a genius is a super smart jerk.

She'd read and read. Not just what to expect when she was expecting, but what kind of shit show might follow.

While Freddie nurses, she muses some more on the daemon/genius thing. The Christians turned it into some guardian angel who presses a fingertip into the divot above your lip, your philtrum—maybe she should call Freddie *Phil*—and promises to Watch Over You. The Greeks, or at least Socrates or Plato, had a more muscular figure in mind. Daemonic. Bossy. Psychopompy.

No, that might be Freud. Or Jung.

Is this "baby brain"? The thing no one wants to admit is real? She can't keep a thought in her head. It's like the baby is sucking her brain right out of her.

"Freddie," she whispers, "Freddie, who are you?"

He nurses a while before saying, "You are going to have to decide, you know."

"Decide what? Who you are?"

"Guardian angel, daemon, genius. They're not the same thing. You are going to have to decide."

And with that, he shuts up. But the *decide* has come out *dethide*, and his tiny, heavy lids slide a little ways down his eyeballs, rise up again, fall again, a little lower, up, and down all the way. They stay shut. Renee breaks the latch with her fingertip and, in doing so, brushes a patch of toothless baby gum. A tooth is gone. Two.

Maybe he is growing up.

But what does she believe, exactly? If she doesn't know what she believes, does that mean she doesn't believe in anything?

From that moment to the time she falls asleep in the dark, Renee thinks about it.

Next morning, after a slow shuffle to the WC for a pee and a squirt from the peri-bottle, she takes a good look at herself in the mirror. Her reflection shows her post-labour wild hair and blotchy skin, a burst blood vessel on the white of her eye like an exploded peony.

She sees the intelligence, buried deep in her melasma-darkened sockets, altered, she can already tell, permanently. The belief question is annoying her. At first, she thought the answer was simple: she's Christian, of course, in the same way that she's for democracy and probably a capitalist too. They seem about equal in weight.

But now, to her horror, she sees the face in the mirror as the face of a maenad—and why does she even remember what a maenad is? The flat front of her nightgown goes blurry for a moment, becoming a leopard skin; her mouth spreads in a grimace, showing the blood on her sharp teeth, and the peri-bottle is a thyrsus, ready to strike wine from rocks or sons' heads from their shoulders. She squeezes the bottle in alarm, and the squirt strikes the mirror, shattering the image.

"Uh, uh, uh," she says. She wants to wipe off her tongue with toilet paper or a towel. She'd like to wipe clean the surface of the squashy pink cauliflower she pictures her brain to be. She would like to rid it of the crap she learned in that private school, where she nerdily read her way through the classics as though someone were making her. A stupid time, stupidly feeling safe, wadded into a library chair, the ancient Greeks more real to her than her own family and nicer to her than her own, uh, friends.

Yeah, she's read Plato and Hesiod and Homer and a bunch of others: the gods hating each other, going after helpless humans, cows, swans, partridges, anything, walloping each other with the island of Sicily, leg-fucking sleeping goddesses, poking burning branches into the eyes of the one-eyed. None of it as vicious, thinks Renee, as the girls, in their grey uniforms, on the field hockey pitch, or worse, in the middle of the night. She can't stop the unbidden recollection of a night-waking by an upended garbage can full of ice water, and the sight of herself (burned forever into the retina of her mind's eye) sitting straight up in her narrow dorm bed, sodden and so much in shock that she said nothing, only stared at her hands, held in front of her face, as though they might hold a clue as to why this was being done to her. She didn't cry then: too much shock, too much cold. And she didn't cry when she told her mother about it, and she didn't cry when her mother told the headmistress that she, Renee, most certainly would be coming back after the short weekend home. Renee—not to mention Renee's family—would only lose face were they to allow the uncivilized behaviour of others to humiliate them.

This crying, now, she determines, is part of the hormone reversal of becoming not-pregnant, or becoming postnatal. Come to think of it though, Renee hasn't worn a nightgown since private school, and the one she has on now—also picked out for her by her mother and foisted on her as an irrefusable generosity—is very like the one soaked by the upended garbage can of water and ice.

Time to change.

Renee takes her bag from the hospital room locker, preparing to be taken by her mother's driver to the big house and to her old room.

Freddie awakes with a babyish howl, and Renee lets him cry for a moment, noticing he has lost another tooth. More. He looks like he's lost his dentures.

"Good morning to you, sweetness," Renee says.

"Man likes a bit a titty now then," says Freddie with a dirty old man leer.

"Ugh, Freddie, it's like breastfeeding somebody's creepy grandfather," says Renee, struggling with the snaps of the nursing bra. "Can't you just be a baby?"

"Listen," he says, "the talking stops soon. You'll remember it, but dismiss it as your imagination. And you will dismiss that as though it were something other than your connection to the eternal and divine, as though it were not real, and I can go either way, at this point. Already I am starting to forget. Already I have lost all languages except the one we're speaking now."

It is true. He has developed the lisp of the partially dentured.

"Everyone you know will say it was all in your head, and even those mothers whose children spoke to them in every language from the very first, those mothers will dismiss it as imaginary; the dismissal, the very act of violence that forces the silence broken only by wordless squalling. You yourself will attribute it to whatever narcotic we got during labour: Nubane or one of those intra-musculars. The one that they should give to werewolves at the full of the moon."

Silence on both their parts.

"Guess what I'm thinking about," Freddie says with sudden glee.

"What?" she asks cautiously.

"I'm thinking of Odysseus seeking Tiresias," he says.

"I never would have guessed. The Greeks again?"

"Yes, the Greeks!" confirms Freddie. "The fucking Greeks!"

Renee cannot decide which is weirder, a talking baby or a classically educated talking baby or a baby who swears as much as Freddie does.

She sighs. "Tell me."

He clears his tiny throat.

"Odysseus sought out Tiresias in the underworld, the afterlife, because Tiresias could tell him things none other could. Secrets."

"That's it?" asks Renee.

"That's it. A secret."

Renee thinks a moment.

"What secret are you here to tell me?" she says. Her voice has changed, become more formal, lower, and Freddie's voice lowers in return.

"I am here to tell you …" He intones this solemnly, and Renee is not sure that he is not mocking her, matching her tone. He continues: "That life is the joke."

"That's hardly news," Renee says.

"No, don't misunderstand me. A joke consists of the set-up and the punchline. Here's the set-up: you can lead an exemplary life, sacrifice to the gods, do unto others as you would have them blah, blah and all that. Or not. Be a shit. Fuck the gods. Screw unto others. Still just set-up. But the punchline! The punchline … wait for it. Wait for it. It's gonna kill you."

"So you're going to tell me that it's what comes afterward that counts," says Renee, with a bitterness that surprises her. "That our reward is in the afterlife."

"Afterward?" he says. "Oh no. It's what comes before. The set-up is the only thing that counts."

This is the moment when there is a knock-knock on the door.

It's a driver sent by her mother to take Renee and the baby to her home. Renee asks him to give her a few minutes to get ready.

But she is ready.

She and Freddie sit together on the hospital bed.

"It's almost over, right?" she asks.

"Yes," he replies. Then he asks, "She really used that term? Unwed mother?"

"Yes," says Renee.

Renee hasn't told any of it to Freddie, but she isn't surprised that he already knows. Clearly, he knows a lot.

"And that's why she wasn't at my birth."

"Right."

"And we're going to live with her."

"Right."

"I don't believe it."

"Freddie," begins Renee, "it's just that we have no other place to go."

"How old are you?"

"Twenty-seven. Eight."

"Listen," he says. "Women have been giving birth and caring for children on their own since the ancient Greeks."

"It's not that. I know I can do that."

"So why did you get us into this mess, anyway?"

"I wanted to feel part of something."

"Me too."

Here are some other things Renee now finds that she knows: That she does not live in a heroic or heroinic age. All the fear and pity of tragedy have rolled over to plain old fear, the way putrefying gasses roll about in the belly of a dead horse, causing the animal to shift and roll in death, so you catch yourself waving back at the swaying hooves dangling from the animal's skyward-pointing forelegs, wondering, "Why is that horse waving at me?" before you catch yourself and yank your hand back down.

(When that had happened, Renee had experienced, in reverse, the open-mouth smile that Freddie's smile brings unbidden to her face: staring at the stupid dead horse in a field of burrs and thistles, her delighted grin had melted right down her chin.)

What is there in this world that she can offer this child?

Dressing him in little clothes, she is careful not to speak to him, as though he were a flounder, and she had already wasted two wishes.

But then she begins to whisper, "Don't say anything in reply Fredo, but this is what I think you've been trying to tell me. I am thinking you are trying to tell me that you have fallen out of heaven. Say nothing if this is true."

His eyes are staring with the wide, non-rude interest of an infant. He is smiling broadly. There is a wink of white in his lower gums, that's all.

She goes to the door, sticks her head out, and says to her mother's waiting driver, "Please tell my mother that we will not be returning to her home. I will send for my things."

Then she goes back in to her child.

"And I'm thinking," she continues, checking the doorway, expecting in all unlikelihood, her mother to burst in, "that growing up is hard to do. I believe you when you say you were somewhere before you were here, and I believe your implication that you

25

chose to be here with me now, and that what I thought were my choices were more likely yours."

She pulls her eyes from the door to lock them onto Freddie's.

"If I'm right, Freddie, if these things are true, then don't say anything."

He continues smiling, and when she smiles back, his remaining teeth resorb into his pink gums, the Cheshire Cat in reverse. Freddie's toothless smile remains there for Renee, pulling her along. He just smiles and smiles, saying nothing.

This is the story as it unfolded inside the hospital room, at least for Renee.

The doctors and nurses might remember it another way, perhaps in the ordinary way they would remember the ordinary birth of an ordinary baby to an ordinary mother on an ordinary day.

Easter *or* It's All About Me

This girl who spoke to me in the pharmacy line-up, I had seen her a few minutes before in the parking lot when I was unbuckling my two-year-old nephew from his car seat. I noticed her because of what she was wearing: a really nice-fitting, fingertip-length, black leather jacket with a nice belt and a nice collar to it, over a short plaid skirt that showed an inch or two below the jacket, then black tights and big oxfords like fake Doc Martens.

In the drugstore, I pushed my cart, with my nephew in it, around to the pharmacy counter, and there she was. In the parking lot, I had been mostly looking down at her shoes and stockings and skirt, so now I looked up. She had this head of huge, black, frizzed-out hippie hair in the shape of an A-frame cottage, parted in the middle with nothing punk about it, just totally inconsistent with the rest of her look, except for her face, which she turned to me to hiss something that ended, "having a fucking stroke why don't you for fuck's sake fuck off," followed by a loud exhale of rage-breath. All because I had said, "excuse me, excuse me" to her when the spot where she was standing in the line-up turned out to be the natural gap that a normal person pushing a cart carrying a happily self-conversing two-year-old would choose to cut through.

Suddenly, her outfit didn't make sense anymore. That is, it no longer felt like some nonspecific but generous vote in support of my vestigial but hopefully still noticeable coolness. See, when I had seen her in the parking lot, I had experienced a bizarre and possibly illusory sense of approval: approval of her outfit by me, and imagined approval of me by her for approving of her outfit, as though she could somehow tell that I had pogo-danced across the divide between the seventies and eighties, had never gotten over the death of Joe Strummer, and was secretly still cool, without a trace of it being in evidence. That is, I felt that she and I were friends, that we were naturally allied, somehow. So the "fucking stroke fuck off" stuff took me by surprise.

Luckily, I have the skill of appearing attentive to my nephew's happy blather (my sister is a fuck-up and unable to provide really good care, so I spend as much time with him as possible), so I was able to keep it together and pass behind this phony, hippie-punk hybrid abomination as she hissed her face-distorting vitriol into the side of my head, blasting me with a stink-stream like what comes out of a sun-hot inner tube pierced by a nail on a summer's day.

The non-punk dirty faker was glaring at me, so I deked down an aisle where I could see her and she could see me, but where I was shielded by the seniors waiting to use the self-serve blood pressure cuff. I glared back. I wanted to shout, "Ask for the anti-depressants!" but it would have blown my cover as someone's responsible auntie, so I flipped her the finger, wearing my we're-all-friends-here smile. She whipped away with a scowl.

I saw her one more time before I left the store: She had the pharmacist out from behind the counter and was pointing down the aisle at me, her mouth all scrunched up like a, like, you know, a bumhole. Her voice rose when she spotted me, and I heard something about "the authorities," and then I heard the pharmacist say something about how it was a lovely day, and then he was pointing at something on a shelf, trying to distract her, and so I got us out of there fast.

We walked over to the library, a block and a half away. We went over to the lounge part where you can get a coffee, and when I looked up, who should I see but Her! Yes, Her! Her back was to me, and she was talking to someone who looked really bored, so I zipped us away from the coffee bar and toward the children's section. There we played with the toys and looked at picture books longer than I intended because I really didn't want to run into her again.

I was still waiting for the feeling of adrenalin poisoning I normally get from engaging in the repulsively intense level of intimacy required of strangers to be rude to each other in public. I marvelled at how not-terrified I was. Really, in the past, this sort of rage-connection with a complete stranger would have made me feel all shaky and sick to my stomach. But the feeling didn't come, and, after a while, we left the library and made our way to my sister's.

At the basest level, I guess I was just on high alert because of my nephew. You know: Crazy Person in the Building—Be Ready to Run with Child in Arms. I figure, if I'd had to, I could've hung on to my nephew with one hand and gotten one good punch in with the other. I'm not afraid to be too loud or to call for help or to just scream, but the thing is, I am somebody's auntie now, so I am trying to conduct myself with more dignity. I am trying to be more responsible.

I gave the little guy back to my sister so she could put him down for his nap. She was kind of crusty with me for some reason, and her littlest one, about three months old, was really whiny and teething, and the older girl was watching TV way too loud, and I just wanted to get out of there, but instead I took a deep breath and asked if I could use her computer. She just looked at me for a minute like she forgot how to be polite and then said quite rudely, "What?"

So I went ahead without her help or permission or whatever, if she was going to be like that. I put one of the pre-perforated, do-it-yourself business card sheets I found in her desk drawer, under her tax return, into the printer and got to work making some nicely printed notes I could hand out to the faux-punk the next time I saw her.

Because I would. It's a small town. I made ten perfect little cards, with a short text that would inform her, politely but firmly, that if she ever looked at me again when I was with my nephew, I would rip off her head and shit down her neck. I didn't say it in quite those words because I like to believe I have a position in the community of some standing and I don't want to jeopardize it.

The very next day I was at the grocery store, alone this time, because my nephew was at home with my sister. I was pretty sure she was going to let him watch TV all day, but there was nothing I could do about it. I had the business cards in the inside pocket of my jacket. I had ten of them. I don't know why I had ten. I hadn't really thought it through, I guess. But in the grocery store I was wondering about it a little, about why I had printed and brought along ten cards when, you know, if I managed to get one into her hand I would be doing well.

And I found that I was thinking about this and choosing items to put in the cart and keeping an eye out for her all at the same time, and I found, too, that I had this funny and familiar feeling, kind of excited and a little nervous but mostly happy, like anticipatory, and I realized that the feeling I was having was that cholera feeling, and that I had some kind of weird I'm-going-to-get-you crush on this poor girl, who wasn't even a girl at all because she was probably within ten years of my age, if her grumpy tent-around-the-nose-and-mouth lines were any indication, and I couldn't wait to see her again! I was in love.

I finished the groceries as quick as I could and drove home all happy and I've-got-a-mission-y because I had decided I was going to change the message on my cards. I didn't know what I was going to say yet, but it had to be short, to fit on a card, and it had to be accurate. It was a complex message to convey, along the lines of, "You were hideously rude to me in public and I was rude back, but I have figured out you probably have more to be miserable about than I have, and that made me reflect on my good fortune, and so I don't have to get revenge on you, and instead I will just forgive you."

It made me feel good.

I shortened it to "I Forgive You" and printed out ten and put them in my coat pocket.

Later on, I was downtown, kind of looking for this girl and kind of just soaking up the sun's rays and immersing myself in my newfound feeling of love and forgiveness, when who should drive by but this guy I used to be in a band with. No fooling. I had called him up and asked him to play guitar on some songs I was recording, even though I knew he hadn't played in public in a long time, and he agreed to after some persuading, and the bass player and the drummer and the back-up singer were really nice to him, and we did the recording, and then they all went on to form a new band without me.

Now all this flashed before my eyes in the time it took for the light to go from red to green, and in that time he looked out his window—it was open—and saw me and yelled, "Hey we're playing tonight at the X Club, come and see us!" and I thought, "Yeah, right, Fuckypants. Like I'm going to do that in a million years or so," and then the light changed and he drove off.

When I got back to my sister's, I had an idea, so I used her computer to revise the business cards to read, "When our band broke up you asked everyone to join your new band except me, so of course I'm not going to come to your gig," printed a page with five of those and five of "I Forgive You" for the girl, and put them in my pocket for later.

I got to the X Club really early, before the band even got there for the sound check, because I didn't want to miss them, so I hung around and had a rye and Coke. There were these two old guys at the table next to mine. They were both kind of fattish, one of them had on a nice madras plaid button-down shirt with short sleeves, and he was leaning across the table to the other one, who was all kind of sullen looking and slumpy and had hair like he had bought a not very good quality gorilla suit and cut out the face part and just left the head hair as a kind of hat-wig, so he looked like he had maybe a really bad zinc deficiency.

The one in the madras shirt was talking way too loud, and he sort of yelled, "And before I knew it, I had drunk myself all the way to Bolivia!" And I thought to myself, he's the sponsor and the other one's an AA. And I kind of ran the Twelve Steps through in my head, just sort of mentally reading over the list, and when I got to Step Eight, "Made a list of all persons we had harmed, and became willing to make amends to them all," I naturally thought of Step Nine, "Made direct amends to such people wherever possible, except when to do so would injure them or others," and a penny dropped, and I thought, *What I need are direct amends.*

The guy who was all slumped down—the slunchy AA one, not the sponsor—was drinking a drink, not a beer, and I thought, "Hoo, that's going to be a write-off," but I said to the sponsor, "Excuse me, when's your next meeting?" and he got this big smile on his face and said, "Tonight!" and told me where and gave me a little piece of paper with the information all printed on it—my card idea is going to work, I know it—and the meeting was actually starting really soon, so I got up to go and on my way out I said to him, "Hope you liked Bolivia." What a knob.

My idea was to go to the AA meeting and hope that somebody I knew would be there. Most of my ex-friends are alcoholics anyway, and maybe one of them would have gotten their shit together enough to join AA, and maybe if they saw me there and they were around Step Nine, they could come over and give me the apology they so owe me and which I so richly deserve. I could easily help them out in this matter and still make it back to the X Club in time.

The meeting was being held in the Orangemen's Hall, and I took it as proof that I was really living my life On Purpose, that I was on the right path, because right outside the hall was the bicycle of this girl I had shared an apartment with once, and all I had to do was cross the street, go into the hall, and get my apology.

I felt like I had died and gone to heaven: There was a long, tunnelly corridor with a white light at the end of it, and there were all these people waiting to greet me, some of whom I knew, but then over there was Kurt Cobain and also C.S. Lewis who was doing something lewd to a guy who could only have been Jesus, not because I know what Jesus looks like, but because who else would C.S. Lewis blow but the pin-up boy of S/M homos Himself? And over there was Joe Strummer, arguing with Sid Vicious about whether Charles Bukowski had been a Beat poet or not—well, not arguing exactly: it was really mostly Joe ranting and Sid drooling some awful foamy white stuff, and then Joe giving up in disgust and slinking off toward where Bob Marley was rolling fatties the size of dachshunds with John Lennon and Mae West and Robert Mitchum and Montgomery Clift, and I suddenly realized that, in fact, I *had* died and gone to heaven, and I was making a beeline for Joe to tell him that I had named my cat Strummer, when I got this wavy feeling, and then it felt like someone had put a vacuum cleaner nozzle up to my bum and, just as suddenly, I got Called Back. Fuckity.

I was facedown on the street outside the Orangemen's Hall, and my mouth was full of gravel. More accurately, I was in the gutter near the curb because I had rolled there after being hit by the car. I didn't hurt yet, and my arms were tight by my sides and my feet were flat out, toes pointed, like I had died in a layout for a high dive, and I could tell there was something wrong with my nose. I made this kind of *bleee* noise, like a sheep with a sock on its tongue, and tasted dirt and blood. After a while, I could hear sirens. A hand touched my shoulder, and at the same time that I heard someone yell, "Don't turn her over!" someone turned me over, and I was looking up into the face of the girl from the pharmacy. She looked really mad, still: the scrunched up mouth with some of her front teeth showing, and her lips white with how tight she was squeezing them.

I am not a snob, but I figured this girl wouldn't know who Demosthenes was, so I didn't mention it. Besides, when she turned me over, I found I couldn't say—or move—anything: I could blink and *bleee*, but I certainly couldn't feel my feet or legs or hands or arms or butt or anything, and the pebbles in my mouth made me feel like I didn't even have spit, so there was no way for me to tell if I could swallow it or not.

Then the girl did this really strange thing: She knelt down really close to my head and opened my mouth with her hand and cleaned the stones out with her finger, and then knelt in even closer so that her face was practically touching mine, and I could tell she was concentrating, and then she spat into my mouth. Not gobbed or horked, but more like *then she releaseth a stream of saliva to flow from unto her mouth into mine.* And then I could move again. I sat up.

The ambulance pulled up with a screech, and all these white shoes pounded out, and a stretcher went plop beside me. I looked around. The day seemed clear as anything, and I could see the girl in her leather jacket and plaid skirt loping across a lawn and through someone's lilac bushes, hunched over a bit but plainly visible. And I turned my head to the ambulance guys and smiled because I felt happy, and I said, "I'm all right, I'm all right now." They didn't want to let me get up and walk away, but did you know they can't stop you? They made me sign a piece of paper and that was it.

There was a little crowd outside the Orangemen's Hall, like all the AA meeting attendees had come out to see what the fuss was, and the guy with the monkey hair and Bolivia Boy were there, and Bolivia Boy kept saying, "She shoulda been dead. She shoulda been dead. It's like some Higher Power intervened or something, holy crap."

The members of my ex-band were there too, looking all fucked up like they had been driving the car that hit me or something, and, yup, sure enough, there it was: our old band van, with the front mashed in and a hi-hat stand sticking out of the broken windshield like the stem of a corsage with its petals busted up or blown off.

I was standing pretty well now, and I dusted off my jacket a bit and reached into the inside pocket and got my cards to give them each one—Fuckypants, Bolivia Boy, Monkey Hair, all of them—and as I handed them out, I noticed each card now read, "I'm Sorry." I gave one to each of them, but I still had a few left.

Now the whole time I was doing this—it only took a couple of minutes—I was looking toward where the girl had gone into the bushes. I knew that past the lilac bushes was a ravine full of sumac where people like me didn't go, but where—I had heard—they had lots of parties. And as soon as I could, I made a beeline for the lilacs. Strands of the girl's long black hair had snagged in the branches, leaving a well-marked trail for me to follow, and then there was an old split-rail cedar fence, and more of the hair was there and also in the dry rock pile on the other side of the fence, and then clumps of hair on the ground, and I started thinking she would be bald by the time I caught up to her. I was crouch-running as fast as I could, and I still had my cards squeezed in my hand, getting sweaty.

And then I was in the circle of trees. There was poplar and young birch, and I think they must have been planted a while ago—not too long ago, but long enough for the trees to have grown up in a clearly demarcated circle, in the centre of which was a sort of stand for like a scarecrow or something: a pole with a little crosspiece for the feet to rest on and a bar across the top for the arms. And there was the girl, just climbing up onto it and putting her arms into the sleeves of this ratty white shirt that hung on the pole with the bar through its arms. Most of her hair was gone, and she was quiet, and her jacket and skirt were gone, and she was naked, mostly. Her chest was bare, and she had almost no breasts, just very flat, and her flanks were exposed, and I thought, *skinned rabbit*, and she had on some panties. There were now people suddenly coming out of the bush and into the grove, and I thought one of them was going to take the panties off her, and that she was going to be a man, but that didn't happen. Some of the people helped her get her feet onto the crosspiece, and a couple of them used strips of cloth to actually tie her wrists, inside the shirt cuffs now, to the crossbar. These people were all grown-ups, but they were dressed grotesquely in children's clothes: large-sized OshKosh overalls and Batman t-shirts, and the ladies in short dresses with frilly underpants that showed, and they all had wicker baskets in pastel colours in their hands, and some of them were actually skipping around while they put this woman up on the cross, and when she looked at me she said, "Do you think I like this? Do you think I actually like this?"

I found the cards in my hand had gone completely blank. There seemed nothing to do but tear them into little squares and eat them, so I did, one at a time.

I wish my nephew had been there. I would have held him close and whispered to him, "Aren't they nasty, my sweetheart? Aren't those nasty people all nasty?" But instead I just watched.

Dear Dave Bidini

This story is dedicated to the memory of Solomon Northey

Dear Dave Bidini,

I hate hockey, but can we still be friends?

As you can tell, I am a fifteen-year-old boy, and this is true. I lie on my bed and listen to my mom's old albums. I am listening to *Whale Music*, and I feel like you know me even though it was recorded before I was born. Dear Dave Bidini, did you think the world would have changed by now? When you were growing up, did they have trans? I think I am trans. I am not really a boy, but when I think about having sex, I always imagine that I am a boy doing it with a boy.

Dear Dave Bidini, I lied about being a boy. This part is true. Dear Dave Bidini, I hope this is not embarrassing for you.

Solomon is in my algebra class and is called Sol. His parents home-schooled him until this year. Home-schooled kids are supposed to be different and open-minded, so I might be able to be friends with him. Tomorrow I am going to give Sol a note in algebra.

Dear Dave Bidini, I asked Sol if he wanted to come over to my place after school tomorrow. He said yes.

Dear Dave Bidini, Sol is coming over today. He barely looked at me in algebra.

Dear Dave Bidini, Sol will be here in a few hours.

Dear Dave Bidini, I just shaved my head.

Sol didn't mind it. He said he thought it was cool. And when he sat down on my bed to do homework, we did homework.

Dave Bidini, I wish we'd had sex. His skin smelled like rain. When he was reading his textbook, the back of his neck looked very smooth and brown. There were fine hairs on it in the shape of an arrow that pointed to a place that made me want to put my hands down the front of his pants. Are everyone's thoughts this dirty? The backs of Solomon's ears are beautiful.

When he left, I lay on my bed with my hand clamped between my legs. This part is weird, Dave Bidini. I pretended I was Sol and my hand was me. I'm a girl, Dave Bidini, so this is trouble.

My mom came home from work about the time I'd finished making supper. I made hamburgers and frozen french fries and Caesar salad. When she saw my scalp, she didn't say much. She couldn't, exactly, having told me my whole life, "A Mohawk, dear, is always a good fashion choice." She is obsessed with The Clash. But I could tell she didn't like it because she started pulling out hats after supper, asking which one I was going to wear to school tomorrow.

Dear Dave Bidini, today at school Sol ignored me. No one noticed my shaved head, or if they did, they didn't say anything. I wore a hat. No one ever looks at me anyway.

There is a girl in my class who everyone says is a lesbian. I'm not interested in her. The thought of her bust against mine just makes me think of hugging an air bag. It would be soft and squishy, and I would sink into it like it was an air bag on impact, and I would die from the thing that was supposed to save me. I can't even think about what it would be like on her down there. I want to feel my hard chest against Solly's hard chest. I would like the sound of his teeth knocking against mine when we kissed.

Dear Dave Bidini, when I came home from school today, my mother was already here. She was crying at the kitchen table, holding a Polaroid of her mom. She told me she was crying because she was remembering her mom, but that it's not my job to carry her emotions. Yeah right, like she really means that.

When I went into my room, she was still crying. I could hear her. I started thinking about a song I could play for her to cheer her up. I went out to the kitchen and put my iPod buds in her ears, so she could listen to "Record Body Count." Dear Dave Bidini, she just kept crying. I wonder if she has depression.

It's just me and my mom, Dave Bidini. We are a single-parent, single-child family. There was never a father, Dave Bidini. I think he was some guy in a band. It's the only thing that makes sense to me, Dave Bidini: my father was a rock star and my mother was a guitar. I am not some one, Dave Bidini. I am some thing. I feel like a thing, when I listen to music. There is a guitar solo you do in between "Rain" and "Queer" that makes me feel like it is actually being played on my stomach. I feel it on my belly, but not your hand. I feel the notes. It feels great, Dave Bidini, and I could do it over and over again. Most of the time, I do.

When my mom came into my room, she sat on my bed and kissed me and told me she loves me. Then she said, "You should tell people how much they mean to you before they die."

God, she is so creepy sometimes. But I am thinking, Dave Bidini, that I should tell you how much your music means to me before you die. Are you old, Dave Bidini?

Sol again. He came up to me in the parking lot and asked if I could come to his place. His mom was picking him up. I said yes and got in their car with them. I didn't call my mom, Dave Bidini. Not right away.

Sol's house is incredibly cool. There is a live tree growing in their kitchen, in the middle of the table. It comes up out of the floor, and when you go in the basement you see this giant hole his dad must have dug when they built the house. They built the house around this tree.

Sol is very mature for his age and has a great vocabulary and is what my mother would call "emotionally intelligent." When we were sitting on his bed, getting ready to do homework, he told me that he'd always thought I was too cool for him. He said he was intimidated. I thought, *I thought you hated me.*

And then, Dave Bidini, I leaned over and kissed him on the mouth. When he kissed back, I took his hand and placed it inside my shirt but outside of my bra. Sol froze for a sec, like he was startled, but then relaxed but stayed completely still.

Then, after a second, he started moving his hand around. A lot. We did that for a long time, while kissing, first with our mouths closed, but then it was so great my lips kind of opened on their own and a noise came out of me like I'd never heard myself make before.

Sol got up, went to his bedroom door, which was open, and stuck his head out and called, "Mom?" She didn't answer, and he shut the door and locked it behind him.

"Is she gone out?" I asked.

He shook his head. "I don't think so," he said. "She's probably outside stirring the compost. But we've talked about sex, me and her and my dad. They said I should only have sex with people who like me, and that it should be pleasurable. They also said it was better to have the first time here, rather than in the back seat of a car."

"I like you," I said.

Sol took off his glasses, and I unbuttoned my shirt. He put his hands and then his arms around to my back. Then somehow, we were both in our underpants, kissing like crazy. Dave Bidini, we touched each other everywhere, and I didn't feel like a girl or a guy. I just felt like me.

When I got home, I didn't tell my mom I had had sex because, technically, I hadn't. What happened is that I had my crotch against Solly's leg, and the kissing was more like we were eating ice cream out of each other's mouths. It happened, the You Know. For me, anyway. I was dizzy and something beyond happy—like hearing a great guitar solo, but hearing it with my chest, my heart, my body. But there was no sound coming out of me or Solly. No sound from either of us, just this amazing music in me instead of blood or air. Solly's teeth made a little clash against mine, and he pushed his tongue against my tongue so our mouths were apart, and his eyes opened very suddenly, into mine, then squeezed shut just as fast. Solly held on to me so hard I could feel his hard chest against mine, our collar bones sharp on each other's, our foreheads pressed hard together. He made a noise, just then, that has played in my ear ever since. Over and over again, all the time, since yesterday.

Afterward, Solly was a bit embarrassed about the mess, but I said don't worry, I can get you a towel.

I can't wait to do it again. Sol has to go with his parents to Tofino tomorrow, but he's coming over to my place the next day after school, which is Friday, when my mother works late at the radio station!

Now it's tomorrow. Dave Bidini, I think she is cracking up.

I was clearing the table after supper, and out of the blue, she says, "What noises do rock stars make that you like?"

"Huh?"

My mother doesn't understand, Dave Bidini. She thinks that I love you. I don't love you, Dave Bidini, I want to be you. I think that if I had been a boy, Dave Bidini, I would have been you. Is that the same as love?

"It's usually the stuff other than the words and the chords that really pulls you into the song," my mother is saying.

"Like …"

"Like Joe Strummer crowing like a rooster in "London Calling." That's what got me the first time I heard it. I thought, 'What would make him decide to do that?' That's the kind of thing that has always gotten me. And the Beastie Boys—"

"Beastie Men is more like it."

"—uh, and I was just … wondering … if you listen to music that way."

"Well, Dave Bidini does this thing on the guitar that he maybe doesn't mean to, it's not music, it's this noise—"

"Oh, Dave Bidini!" she interrupts me. "I saw him the other day. He was with his kids."

Ohmigod, Dave Bidini. You're still alive. And if you have kids, then you're probably the same age as my mother. And maybe you know each other. She knows lots of rock stars because of her job. But Dave Bidini, are you still the guy whose voice I hear on "King of the Past?" I want to know. Do I love you or the sounds you make, that you make on your guitar? I don't want to be a rock star, Dave Bidini, but I do want to know why I love you the way I do.

"Tell me more about what you listen for in a song," I ask my mom. I can tell she's happy, because I don't usually seem very interested in what she has to say. I am, but I don't show it, and she can't tell, so she usually seems disappointed and tries to hide it.

"Oh, I like the squeaks and the feedback and the scraping sound the guitarist's fingers make when they skate up the strings during a solo, almost as much as the solo itself, and I like those things that singers mutter close to the mike when they're not singing, but they decide to keep them on the record anyway. And the breathing, the inhales. And I like real drums. You didn't have to live through the 80s thank God—those stupid drum machines were as perfect as laugh tracks."

I am drifting a little bit, and she is going off in her own world, all happy to be talking about rock and roll, and about herself. She's a really good mom, Dave Bidini, but she's different.

"I'm going to have sex here tomorrow with Solomon Mellor," I say.

There is a very long pause.

"I thought you'd like to know. You always said I should tell you, that I could tell you."

"I see. Thank you."

"We'll probably get some, some. Get some, um—"

"We need to talk about birth control."

Thanks, Mom, I think at her. But instead I say, "We're going to get some condoms."

"Is this the first—uh, should you have been on the pill, or the patch? Before this?"

I can't bring myself to say anything.

"I, uh, I thought—" she begins.

"You thought I was a fucking queer."

Now she says nothing.

"Everybody does, just because I don't wear my underwear on the outside of my clothes or have a word on my pants you can read off my ass."

Neither of us has ever really heard me talk like this, and we're both kind of shocked, I guess.

"I guess you're right," she says. "I did think maybe you were gay."

Then she says, "Look, it doesn't matter to me if you're straight or gay or what. You know that."

I do know that. She would probably be thrilled if I were, so that she could be the first parent in our building to start a chapter of PFLAG.

"You've told me a few times," I say.

"What's important is that the boy is nice to you, and that you only do what feels good for you."

"You sound like a hippie."

"A what?" She is totally horrified.

"I know this kid whose mom is a hippie, and she told him the same thing."

"Mmmm. Mmhm," she says. When she stops using words and just uses sounds I know she is offended and trying not to be.

"Maybe punks and hippies aren't that different," I say.

"Oh my God," she says.

"Like, nobody even uses those words anymore," I say. "Hippie, anyway. And punk doesn't seem to mean much. Or maybe too much. I don't know."

"Would you call yourself a punk?" she asks.

"No way," I say.

She looks at me. I want to change the subject.

"The Clash—" she begins.

"Weren't even punk by *London Calling*," I finish, and then there is a long, *long* pause.

"I guess you're right," she says.

"Look," I say, "out of all the parents I know, except maybe Solly's, you are still cool."

I don't tell her Solly's parents are hippies. That tree in the house.

"Sweetheart," she says, "I am so glad you think so. But you cannot imagine how much I have sold myself out."

"What are you talking about?" I ask. "You work at a radio station, you do all that stuff for the NDP, your hair is blue, and you buy all that Nicaraguan fair-trade coffee."

"Strummy," she says, which is her nickname for me from when I was small. She calls me Strummer now, all the time, which is better, but the kids at school generally call me Bummer, and I am going to ask Solly to call me by my middle name, Patti. Short for Pattismith. God.

"Strummy," she says, "I have not lived up to my own ideals. It's a hell of a realization when you reach my age."

And she pauses here, then adds, "But my disappointment and sense of failure is not your burden, *capisce*?"

See what I mean about how she puts her shit on me all the time, and then says that she isn't? I know she tries to understand me, but I don't want to have to understand her. That's just too much.

"Look," I say, "so you're not a punk either, even though you were thirty years ago, or whatever it is—"

"Twenty-five."

"Twenty-five. But you still believe what you believed in then, don't you? I mean, you told me that being punk in those days was about wanting to change things, not just bitch about it. DIY. All that."

"And?"

"And that's kind of what hippies were like, right? Only in the sixties?"

"Highly debatable, but the idealism of protest music, which punk was, and folk music, as in Woody Guthrie—*folk* here referencing outsider music, or marginalized music that speaks truth to power, making Johnny Cash the first American punk— "

"Mom?"

"Wha?"

"If I think about talking to or writing to someone who made an album twenty years ago, and that someone is alive still, what does it mean?"

"It means you are talking to or writing to who that artist was when they made the album."

"Okay. Good," I say.

"I mean, are you going to be the same person you were twenty-five years ago?"

Huh?

"Am I the same person I was twenty-five years ago? Well, yes and no."

"I thought so."

There's another pause while she looks at a spot in the air above my head.

"So, if I called you a hippie, Mom, I didn't mean it in a bad way. More like some of the hippie ideas were like your punk ideas, and that makes *hippie* better, okay?"

"Okay."

We're quiet again, and I'm thinking about you, Dave Bidini. Are you still the guy who wrote "Beerbash"?

My mom says, "So now I am indistinguishable as a punk. Ex-punk. I could be an ex-hippie, even."

"Mom," I say, "are you okay with me and Solly having … you know … here. Tomorrow night?"

"I guess I always hoped we'd have that kind of relationship when you grew up, I guess, where you'd feel okay about talking to me about this, I guess. I mean, I tried to raise you so that you would feel—"

"Okay. I'm telling you."

"Okay. I'm glad. Yes. I'm glad you told me."

"Okay."

"I'll be home late."

"Okay."

She gets up to go do something.

"Mom," I say, "I'd rather be raised by an ex-punk than an ex-hippie."

"Why?" she says with a smile that says she doesn't believe me. "Because of all my radical ideals that have flabbed out around my butt into hippieness? Because almost none of what I believed in came true?"

I don't quite know what to say to this.

"Listen, Pattismith—" she starts in, remembering to use my middle name this time, which I suddenly realize sounds incredibly lame—I might have to go back to Strummy. And I guess I make some kind of sound, because she repeats herself.

"Pattismith," she says again, doing one of her big-deal inhales, but this time she surprises even me with her big deal. "Having a lot of ideals is like having only a bit of talent. You expect too much and like yourself too little …"

"No," I say. "The whole punk thing … just better music. I mean, no love songs. So you can make that part up yourself, without someone telling you how you're supposed to do it. Feel it. Do it."

Without a word, my mom gets up and kisses me. Squeezes my face, looks at me really hard, looking at me like she's super happy and like she is going to cry, so still kind of weird and sad. She kisses me again, then goes out of the kitchen.

Dave Bidini, I can hardly wait until the day after tomorrow. But now that you're real, I'm not going to write to you anymore.

And even if I did, Dave Bidini, even if I did, when you read this it won't be me who's telling you the story that I'm telling you right now.

Spontaneous Generation

It ended badly for the bird in the chimney, possibly worse for the generations that sprang from it.

But let me back up, closer to the beginning.

We heard thrumming from behind the glass doors of the fireplace. It sounded bottled. A closed system, sealed at both ends. But how could that be? It was open at the top.

The first time the sound came, my son whispered, "Thunner."

"Not thunder. A bird." We listened.

I couldn't get the flue open. Even if I could, what was I going to do? Stick my head in the chimney and shout, "Up! Up!"?

I jabbed around inside with a poker, thinking *birdbrain.*

"Will it get in the house?" my son asked.

"No, honey," I lied. "The bird will fly back up the chimney."

"To its family?"

"Yes."

"To its nest?"

"Yes."

"Is it a baby?"

"No, sweetheart."

"Is it a dad?"

"Yes, honey."

"Does it have babies?"

"Yes."

"Will it fly up to its babies?"

"Yes."

"Is there a mom?"

What happened next was that the phone rang.

It was my sister calling, which was surprising. She told me she was going to be at a conference near my home, which was also surprising since her job had never taken her out of province before and she had never visited before. She hadn't even called me on the phone in years.

See, there's an eleven-year age difference between us, she being older than me. And while we had enjoyed some episodes of closeness, they were separated by long periods of, well, separation.

Even more surprising, I found myself saying with no hesitation, "You have to come visit! I'll pick you up. No, no! It's not too far. I do it all the time. I mean, not all the time—only when I'm getting someone from the airport. Do I drive there. To the airport. I don't mind. Really. When do you fly in? Yes. See you then."

I hung up.

"Was that the mom?"

"Hmmm?"

"Was that the mommy bird on the phone, calling to say she was coming?"

"Oh. No, honey. It was my sister."

"You have a sister?"

"Let's listen to the bird."

Over the next few days, I cleaned the house and thought about my sister and about the times we had called each other since I left home and about the fewness of those times. The thrumming in the chimney came less and less and lasted for shorter and shorter periods.

"You could call an exterminator," my husband offered. "A bird in the house is bad luck."

But I didn't, and finally it was quiet. I didn't have to think about bad luck because, technically, it was a bird in the *chimney.*

"Is the bird still in the chimney?" my son asked.

"No, honey, it got out."

"Will it come back?"

"I don't know, honey."

"How did it get out?"

"It flew."

"Out the top?"

"Yes."

Did it learn to fly vertically, grating its wing tips to dust on the rough brick inside the chimney? Did it come to believe that the universe is long and narrow, curving in on itself and dark, always dark? I decided to tell myself that it had found its way up the chimney, out the top.

What likely happened, though, is that it died a slow, terrified death, trapped and starving. Or asphyxiating or something. But it wasn't me. I mean, I wasn't trying to kill the bird; I wasn't even thinking about it, really. Once in a while I might think *thunner*, but then it would pass, and I would forget again.

I drove the two hours to the airport, picked up my sister, turned around, and drove back.

The next morning, while we were sitting in the kitchen drinking coffee, the long march was first observed.

A trail of white, fat, semi-translucent grubs was humping slowly from the hearth to the patio doors.

"My goodness," said my sister, not getting up and taking a sip from her cup. "Where are they coming from?"

I had not told her about the bird in my chimney. I had kept it in the back of my mind on the drive, in case I needed it for a conversation starter, but we found things to talk about. It had been, after all, years since we'd seen each other.

Now her reaction to what was clearly a row of maggots making its way across my living room floor made me feel that I hadn't put her off too much during the two-hour drive from the airport, even though I had yammered nervously from the moment I put her suitcase in the trunk, trying to reveal all my pathetic, neurotic eccentricities, but in a fun way, so that she would know what she was in for. I figured I easily had enough material for 120 minutes, but what happened instead is that in the first conversational blank, she mentioned our cousin. Since her mouth and eyes narrowed when she said the words, "Robert called me," I blurted in response, "He molested me when I was little." Robert was an older cousin to me, a younger cousin to her.

She didn't look at me or say anything; she was silent. Then, squinting at the windshield, she said flatly: "The next time I see him, I will cut his heart out."

There was more silence after that. Traffic was heavy, and I was concentrating on driving. She had never been through Toronto before. Looking out the window and reading road signs and store names, she said, "Look! Miracle Mart. Let's go buy a miracle." And we both laughed.

I had not told anyone in my family about my cousin before, and we did not speak of it again, finding plenty to talk about driving in the night.

And so now, this morning, the long march: with my little boy having a nap, my husband at work, and a maggot parade at our feet, we finished our coffee and made a plan.

The fact that she did not leap up or shriek, but rather allowed her delighted curiosity to show on her face, made me love her, suddenly.

We killed all the grubs that day, with paper towels and toilet paper, making it a contest to see who could get the most, marvelling at how many kept coming and coming and coming. It was surprisingly fun to have maggots.

What was not so fun was when they returned two days later.

"I thought we got them all!" my sister cried. "Get the paper towels."

Squashing and wadding, I confessed: "Uh, I think a bird died up the chimney a couple weeks ago."

We squashed together in silence for a while, long enough for me to ponder the inanity of my remark. I mean, would she make the connection between a dead bird up my chimney a few weeks ago and the maggots on the floor now? So I cried, "Thus disproving once again the theory of spontaneous generation!" as though in explanation.

You'll know, of course, that I was referring to the pre-Enlightenment belief, held by natural philosophers, physicians, barbers, and priests, by dying milkmaids and ailing queens, by everyone really, that rats and maggots and other creeping things erupted spontaneously from mud and nightsoil, like Athena springing fully formed from Zeus's head. Then, at the end of the seventeenth century, Antonie van Leeuwenhoek figured out how to craft lenses small enough to lead to the invention of the microscope, and the truth was out: nothing comes out of nowhere. Baby rats came out of bigger rats, butterfly larvae out of tiny butterfly eggs, flies out of maggots. And although van Leeuwenhoek later revealed blah blah blah, and I'm blathering because, you see, I have a head for these things; I can forget about a bird dying in the chimney, and I can forget to call home for years at a time, but I can remember the history of science that I learned in grade nine.

Therefore I was thrilled when my sister laughed heartily at my spontaneous generation joke, and I marvelled again that we had anything in common at all, much less obscure references to discredited scientific theories, because although my sister and I have the same parents, I am not sure we were raised by the same people. Part of it is the age difference, of course. Were my parents at twenty-three—the age they were when my sister was born—the same people they were at thirty-four, when I was born? I have seen photographs of us as infants: my sister was scrawny, big eyed, and alarmed looking; as a baby, I was fat and solemn.

I remember my parents as full of rage. Mostly, it was for each other. "Kiss my ass!" my father would cry, storming out of the room. "Move your nose first!" my mom would parry, taking a haul off her cigarette and spouting smoke out triumphantly, tilting her head back to jet it straight up. Always: they were mad at each other, I was mad at my mom, my dad was mad at me. My sister moved out when I was eight and she was nineteen. She married soon after and lived nearby.

So why would I expect her to get my joke about spontaneous generation, about van Leeuwenhoek the lens-grinder and how he brought to their knees all the righteous believers by observing what they could not? Even Isaac Newton said maggots are generated out of meat.

See? You remember Newton, but not van Leeuwenhoek. Yet it was his invention that made it possible for them to do what they were all trying to do: find out how the plague started and stop it, once and for all.

"These will be the maggots feeding on the bird, then," said my sister. "You'll have to get it out of there."

"Look," I cried, pointing. "They're different from last time. Each one has a black spot in it that's ... that's ... WIGGLING!"

"They're fly larvae! That's what maggots are!" my sister shouted, pinching the fleeing grubs.

"Oh my god, this is disgusting!"

We had just erased the trail and all its traces, when my damp-faced little boy thumped down the stairs, the sheen of sleep on his skin, sleepy eyed. Without a word, he padded over to my sister and laid his head in her lap.

"Hello, little man," she said, matching the enormously casual acceptance he had just conferred upon her, smoothing his hair. "Did you have a good sleep?" He was meeting his auntie for the first time on this visit, but he trusted her. She is tender and sure with him, the way she was with her own children and the way I try to be with mine now.

We can do that, in my family. We are capable of great kindness. But sometimes I rage at him, little as he is. Then it's hard to say which of us is more frightened, when my best is not good enough, when it's hopelessly inadequate, and the damage gets done.

We don't tend to be drinkers or drug takers in my family, but we are all addicts, anyway: we are addicted to rage. Of course, we try to balance it out with our capacity for kindness, but it is a questionable sort of kindness. At our best, with a good enough cause, we are righteous bullies.

Once, when I was in grade nine, I went to visit my sister where she was living, in a nearby condo. It had a pool, and my sister and I lounged on towels while some kids who lived in the condo swam. There were three of them, all about twelve or thirteen. My sister and I mostly ignored them, but it became apparent after a while that the girl who was from the reserve was being harassed by the other kids.

"Go back to the reserve, ya wagon burner," was the line, I think, that proved impossible to ignore.

My sister leapt to her feet. She is a physically powerful person: small, compact, and muscled. Even the muscles in her face were flexed, and her eyes were dark as she exploded, "No, *you* go home, you little sons-a-bitches. *You* get out of here. *You* don't belong here. Get out of here. Go!"

Her arm whipped out, pointing toward the gate. Possibly to their own surprise, the boys hauled themselves out of the pool. They shuffled out the gate, dripping.

I remember being impressed, mostly, that she had pluralized *son of a bitch* on the fly. We did not watch the boys go, and we continued to ignore the girl.

See? Kindness.

In my working life, I am a professional righteous bully. On the side of good. I am an advocate for the rights of children. When I am dealing with parents, I am both compassionate and frightening. I tell them that I know they are doing their best, but that their best might not be good enough. I tell this to the ones who just can't or won't protect their young, and sometimes I wish I could scare them into doing better.

And so I appear their champion. Even as I feel something come twisting out of me to claw crookedly at the innocent air, and even as I feel that I am part of a closed system, dark, curving in on itself, but infinite, I am thinking to myself: a righteous bully with a good enough cause. Lucky me.

Shortly after the pool incident, my sister's husband got work in another city, and they moved away. I too left home not long after that, getting out by eighteen.

Other than some intermittent phone calls, that was one of the last times I had contact with my sister. Until the maggot visit.

Two days after the maggots, I drove my sister to the city for her conference and we said goodbye, promising it would not be another ten years until we saw each other again. I went home and called an exterminator. Some young guy showed up and charged a ridiculous price to put on the kind of rubber gloves I use to wash dishes, so that he could open the fireplace flue and let the decomposing body of the bird drop onto a grocery bag spread out on the bottom of the firebox.

"Did you get them all?" I asked.

"All what?" he asked back.

"The maggots. The fly larvae."

"Doubt it," he said. "Two flies can reproduce over 190 billion flies in less than four months."

I told him about my hard work with the wadding and the squashing.

"Well, you would have got some of them," he said, snapping off his yellow gloves like a cleaning-lady surgeon.

"Some?" I said.

"Wash the firebox out with Javex. That should get some of them. At least the smell should go away," he said.

"Smell?" I said, sniffing. "Some?"

He shrugged.

By the time my little boy woke from his afternoon nap, I had wiped out the inside of the fireplace with bleach. I had reached my arm up into the flue as high as I could. Not as high as I was able, but high as I dared: there was the noise from inside the chimney, again. Again or still. The noise of those flightlessly beating wings was horrible and liquid, closed and internal, and seemed to be something I heard not with my ears but with some other part of me. I heard it with an inner ear, like it came from inside of me.

But what happened next is that an unusually large number of very tiny flies began buzzing around the inside of the windows. Friends who came to visit noticed.

"Yes, isn't it weird? It must be because it's so mild out. They were hibernating, and the warm weather has woken them up. Some sort of mid-winter population explosion. They must be getting in through the windows."

It was easy to catch and kill them. I could pinch their tiny wings between my fingers and drop them into the toilet or simply brush them off the windows into a tissue. They seemed sleepy.

By the third wave the flies were larger. Without a microscope, I could observe that their legs were uneven. Of the six they were supposed to have, at least three would be bent like safety pins. They were easy to catch, moving slowly, taking flight only in desperation, when it was clear they would have to let go of the glass in order to escape. When they did, they plummeted to the floor, buzzing wildly on their backs, crooked legs tangling in the air.

I spent a couple days brushing them to the floor and vacuuming them up. But I felt the weight of great scientific discovery and so called my sister. Who else was I going to tell about the disgusting, fascinating, revolting biogenetic experiment I had going on in my house?

"They're back," I said to my sister, over the phone. "But they're mutants. An unleashed horde of cripples, progeny of the bleached larvae."

"Bleached?" she asked.

"I Javexcd a batch of babies a while back," I told her.

"Keep me posted," she said grimly, as if we were hunting serial killers.

We were calling again, a flurry of calls with almost nothing to their substance, but so what? Not like last time there had been a flurry, years after I had left home, during my self-imposed exile. When her husband was leaving her and coming back and leaving her and coming back. She told me they never fought in front of the kids, but I knew that that didn't matter, that the kids knew what was going on anyway, and I told her this repeatedly.

The final call late at night, my sister telling me in a frantic, sobbing whisper that her husband was outside the house. Either he had no key, or my sister had changed the locks, I don't remember which. He had a gun. She could see the long barrel when she looked through the dark window, and he said so, he said so, when he banged on the door.

"You have to call the police," I said. But she couldn't.

From 3000 miles away, I phoned the RCMP unit in her small town, and as soon as I gave the name of my brother-in-law, the Mountie on the line said grimly, "I know him."

What is it about us? What would make my sister marry a man like that? A predisposition to love that is expressed as fighting, legacy of the battlefield of our parents' marriage? A longing for the deep, familiar intimacy of enmity? Just what is this thing that we have in common?

"How interesting," she repeated. "But did you get them all? Do you think you've stopped it?"

"I don't know yet," I told my sister. "I guess we'll have to wait and see."

I was thinking about the next generation of flies and about luck: how it takes a long time, sometimes a generation or more, to find out if the luck you've had has been good or ill, if your hopeless best has miraculously turned out to be good enough, if you've managed to get someone safely out of the pool, if the gunman in the dark goes away bitter, but not a murderer, if my little boy will grow up to be a father, and if he will hurt his children the way I hurt him.

I will have to wait and see, with my son, with *his* children, if luck has been with me and if luck will be with him.

That's how long I'll have to wait and see.

Dog Story

In a house not far from the river, a woman rises from her midnight bed. The moon is a sliver of candy rattling in the ice-hard box of the sky.

From the bed where her husband goes on sleeping, the woman rises, goes to the window, forces the cold sash up, and steps out onto the roof.

In the street below, a dog, dirty white and deeply muscled, a little bug-eyed, stands in yellow lamp light where it is quiet. In the blue outside the lamp light, the exciting smells of the dog's universe are both sharper and more distant than in daylight.

Smoke from a wood fire thrills the dog, vibrating it with dog joy. The odour of food scraps in a compost heap is heard as a complex harmony, suddenly cut through by the scent of a tom spraying its own squint-eyed ecstasy on an abandoned lawn chair. The smells layer themselves in a sense-wrenching symphony of odour. The dog cannot move for the incredible love it feels. Love and smell are identical. The dog stands in the pool of light, love trembling its legs.

The woman's smell plays over the top of the dog's symphony, a high note in a pure sustained line, marvellous in its complexity: the laundered cotton of her nightdress, the damp warmth of her underarms cooling rapidly in the night air, the breath in her mouth, soured slightly by sleep.

The dog, eyes squeezed shut against this beauty, raises its nose to the elegant soprano smell of the woman. She treads on a piece of flashing, and some soft skin from the ball of her foot remains behind, clinging to the metal. The tearing is silent and unfelt by the woman. To the dog, it is an explosion of scent: a piccolo, a silver trumpet, a trilling of bright percussion. Night-red eyes fly open; the dog confronts the source of its joy. Involuntarily, it releases a small amount of urine, and whimpers. The woman is descending upright through the air with her pink hands and feet pointed to the earth. Her stately trajectory describes a slight curve, carrying her into the lamp light, and the dog's good animal wisdom tells it to lie down and play dead.

The woman alights beside the prostrated dog. Fingers rigid, she makes a precise puncture in the dog's abdomen, slits the animal open from breast bone to pubis, and enters.

The dog surrenders its life with the passion of a saint. As the woman dons the animal's hide, the dog begins a dream of a thousand cats. The dream will never end.

The woman roams the backyards of the neighbourhood, rolls in something at the base of a tree. Colours are different from what they were before: the spectrum is narrower, but the varieties of black and white, the subtleties of grey, are alarming and nearly infinite. The dense shadow beneath a bush pulsates with secrets, with promised bliss. Flecks of black mica in the granite stones of a garden wall dazzle the eye, brighter than diamonds. A late-autumn glaze of frost on fence tops is erotic, silver against the night.

In the morning, a man—the woman's neighbour—finds an empty nightdress by the bank of the river. He finds it caught in some low branches where he has been looking for his dog.

When I climb out of the icy river, onto the bank, my nightgown is gone. It was a risk to leave it there like a waving flag, though a

64

lesser risk than entering the water, black and smooth here above the dam, unfrozen and irresistible. The refracted moonlight on the water was more than I could bear, a promise of bones glittering beneath the depth, white and covering the river bed, tasty beyond imagining. I plunged in, thinking that if I could swallow enough moonlight I would get those yummy bones. I snapped my jaws as though maddened and howled with joy, water cascading from my chops. Standing stiff-legged in the water, I plunged my head in up to my shoulders, then my whole body, and the tug of the current was a caress without beginning or end. An endless stroke that smoothed my coat and the skin beneath my coat, rippling. And then scrambling up the bank from the cold water—the joy of four legs! My strength! Shaking myself in an arcing spray, I made a mockery of the stars.

The woman, whose name was Faith, was married to a man called Rex. Lately, Faith had taken to stroking her hairless skin very lightly with her fingertips in spots where every lover she had ever had had marvelled at its softness. Faith found they were right, and this pleased her. That is, she was pleased by her lovers' accuracy. The softness beneath her fingertips was surprisingly silky and pleasant to touch, although the pleasure was felt by her fingertips, and not by the surface of her body on those places her lovers had loved to pet and stroke.

This was a mild puzzle for Faith, whose mind was of a turn to transform nearly everything into metaphor or a symbol used to build a metaphor. Then she would puzzle out the hidden meanings behind the symbols and metaphors she had built, in order to "get at the truth of it." This required of Faith an alert and complex life of concealed invention, which she settled for, it being the least boring way she knew of being in the world.

So the puzzle for Faith was why, if her skin felt so soft to whatever hand touched it, did Faith not feel back a softness from the touch of the world, where the world touched her, where her outside border, her frontier, met the universe. There must be some measurable point, some precise co-ordinate, where the density of her, the specific gravity of her Faithness, must make contact with not-Faithness without dissolving or merging into it. Why was there no perceivable sensation where the collision occurred; why was there, for Faith, no difference that she could detect, where outside becomes in?

I spot my missing nightgown, but I am beyond caring. I want to run, and I run without question, shouting, *hey! hey! hey, hey!* until I am hoarse, but I keep on barking anyway, crying, *hey! hey! me! me!* to a Labrador standing stupidly on its lawn. *Hey!* the Labrador finally shouts back, but I'm long gone. *Hey, hey! I, I, I, me!* I run until I'm back, well, home, for want of a better word. Anyway, I'm here, and Rex is here, and so is our neighbour Whitney Cliff, whom Rex calls Shitney Sniff. The epithet is truer, I realize, than Rex ever suspected. But Rex smells tantalizingly himself and his crotch is emitting wave upon wave of inviting scent. The waves come thick and fast upon each other. I dig my nose into their source.

"Dinah! Dinah! Down! Down, bad dog. Where have you been?" This is Whitney, who is trying to choke me. I hadn't noticed the collar until now. He twists it so cruelly I think I will die. And the humiliation: two squirrels in a tree screech and jeer at me. A robin, embarrassed on my behalf, turns its back and flies away. I can follow only a little of its three-dimensional grammar, as it gestures an expression of sorrow on a vertical plane before turning it into a horizontal lament. The guide feathers of its tail are bent in contempt, betraying its true feelings to me, giving lie to its kind words. I can just make out what it said from afar: sad footer, poor stupid sad footer.

Whitney chains me to a spike in his yard, as though he owns me as a slave. I plead, try to explain, argue, beg, even try to reason with him. He raises a hand to me. My body cowers, my belly pulls itself down to the ground, and I lie there mute, shifting my haunches nervously. I yawn and pant.

I listen at a distance as Rex and Whitney discuss the missing Faith. Rex presses Whitney for details of the nightdress. Rex is truly, touchingly distraught. I feel sympathy for him, but more strongly, I revel in the note his anxiety brings to his sweat. It is a metallic tone, suggestive of blood in the mouth when one bites down on something that has been dead a while. The smell is far better than the taste. I inhale Rex's anxiety. I feel love for him in a way I never have before, a single-minded devotion. When he goes into our house, I leap up and call out to him, *My heart is breaking! My heart is breaking!* I squeeze my eyes shut to hold the little picture of him in my head. My heart is breaking my heart is breaking my heart is brea—I am dreaming of a long-legged chase through the woods at night, the trees lit white as marble by the moon. It is like I am running through a forest of marble pillars and then I am, and I am atop a white horse, galloping, and I am the queen of all dogs. I ride a horse. A fat brown rabbit shows its frightened white backside, zagging away, and I am on it, leaping from the back of the horse, landing with my jaws open on the rabbit's neck. Rabbit fur on my tongue. I bite the creature gently while it kicks out the last squirtings of its heart. Pause for ecstasy: the bursting of flesh, the sound made by silk when it's torn, the jaw's passion. I was made for this. And as I crunch small bones like candies, I see in the grass beside me a little golden crown. Oh! I have kicked myself awake. Dogs dream of chasing rabbits.

I shake the dream off my shoulders and grin without pleasure. I am thirsty. And cold. I dig a bit. I call repeatedly for Rex, and even Whitney. They ignore me. I think maybe Rex has left the house through a door I can't see. Finally, Whitney approaches just as the sun is setting and puts before me a dish of something disgusting. I eat it anyway, as fast as I can. When I finish eating, Whitney unsnaps my collar from its chain, and I bolt into my yard, Rex's yard. I am sure it is my yard, yet to all appearances I live with Whitney. I bark at Rex's back door. He has left. Whitney is calling, "Dinah! Dinah!" He must think it is my name. Perhaps he's right. I'm not sure. It hardly matters. I race down the street, away from his voice, toward the river.

Through the park along the river, I run for the joy of it. I detour into an alley, surprising yowling cats. I leave them behind, frozen in their tracks, with their backs arched impossibly and their hair electrified. I run up the middle of a street, and dart in front of a turning car. Animal squeal of brakes. The driver hates me. He looks like he might have a heart attack. I laugh and keep running. I run into the darkness, and my fear runs with me as my most exciting companion, my guide. My fear tells me where danger lurks and tells me to dare it. Sometimes I say yes and leap over points of cruel wrought iron. Sometimes I snarl *fuckoff* and make a sharp turn away from where my fear tries to lead me. Left feet pirouetting simultaneously, I will my body into a mid-air right angle, use my tail as a rudder, miscalculate, blow it, crash, and somersault. I'm down, so rest. I pant happily, smiling at everything. It is full dark.

Oh! My body is curving itself, forcing me to my feet. My back curls into an unlikely comma, and I strain. I am vaguely embarrassed. What if someone is watching? Close eyes. Squeeze. Relief.

Suddenly I hear another dog nearby. It speaks once sharply, a name, perhaps my name. I straighten, watch it trot toward me and accept its intimate nose. I nose back. My body knows its scent, and we trot off together to a hilltop nearby where other dogs wait. Excited greetings, happy sniffings all around. I sit back, and the half husky, half beagle who has lead me here begins to sing.

At first it is a simple song, *moon, moon, oh moon, white moon, yellow moon,* and some of the other dogs cry, *yes!* or *moon! moon!* in response. Some shout *hey!* or *me!* Shyly, I raise my voice with theirs. When we sing together, I find my voice is round as the moon. I am filled with it. I love to sing.

Then the soloist begins. It is a sad song, but sung without self-pity, and the other dogs howl in agreement and recognition. It sings—the grief of the dog … is that it eats its friends … has only appetite to blame … for loneliness. It is a song about a cat, once loved. The other dogs nod sagely as the song expresses regret and inevitability.

I think of the rabbit in my dream, with its sycophant's smile and triangular skull. A rabbit is an always-frightened creature, but holds its face expressionless in an effort of dignity or invisibility. As though to convince one of its niceness. As though its niceness will protect it. As though it is too nice to be eaten. I am nice, I am sweet, so don't eat me, don't eat me. But bunny, if you are so sweet, I must eat you. A bunny whimpers, *why do dogs do evil to me?* The question rather, sweet rabbit, is why is there evil to be done? I find I have been humming or whining or whimpering the song of it without quite realizing it, and the other dogs are listening now, waiting. I growl and snap the hunt, barking, crunching, gorging. The other dogs laugh, excited. I have gotten their blood up. I do not sing the golden crown. I sing the dead rabbit. The others bark and whistle their applause.

When the applause fades, the terrier-beagle cross called Evey asks me my name. I know it's not Dinah. Why does the word Faith fill my mouth? I hesitate. I think of not running free at night, free of fear. No—not free of fear, but with my fear. Give up the joy of four legs, and a sense of smell and vision more complex by far than anything possible for a human? For a human only seems complex, but in truth is very simple. Feed me. Love me. Foremost, love me. While we dogs … feed me or don't. I can fend for myself. But also love me love me love me, too …

I have waited too long, and the other dogs grow suspicious. *You must guess*, I cry and set off running. I expect the others to give chase. One or two have raised their hackles and start down the hill, but the singing has already resumed on the summit, and these curs merely shout at me over their shoulders as they climb back up. I run through the park unmolested. At my home, I curl on the doorstep where the smell of Rex is strongest and sleep.

"Dinah! Dinah, goddamn what the hell is this?" Whitney is tugging at my collar again and shaking a stinking furry mess at me.

Rex appears at the door, looking terrible. His face is pressed as though he has slept in a vise. Gripping my collar, Whitney talks to Rex, apologizing for the noise, asking for news of Faith. Rex shakes his head once, silent, and lights a cigarette. He kneels down and ruffles the fur around my neck, digging deep under the collar. "Who's in the kitchen with ya, huh, ya bad dog?" he asks me. "Who's in the kitchen with Dinah, Dinah?"

I lick his face, answering that he is delicious, that's what I know.

"What did she find, Whitney, a rabbit?" Whitney holds out the soft, limp body. "Maybe it's somebody's pet."

There is a long, long pause in their talk while I try not to think. I run in tight circles around their legs to distract them. Rex is thinking. Whitney glares at me and I retreat to the lawn. I twist around, letting them think I think I can catch my tail. I can, of course, but I don't. Rex laughs. "Stupid dog," says Whitney.

"The cops want her, Whitney."

Whitney gapes, "Faith?"

"No," Rex makes a small smile.

"Dinah. You said how she's always down to the river, right where you found Faith's nightgown. They asked me if your dog could scent the nightgown and follow a trail." He drags his cheek with his hand. "Think she can?"

"Naw, I doubt it. Too dumb, that one."

"Yeah, I thought so," Rex answers.

I trot over to him. "You're a dumb pooch, aren't ya, honey? A dumb pooch." I put my forepaws on his chest and smile into his eyes.

"Get down, Dinah, you idiot dog." Whitney pushes me.

I can do anything, I say to Rex. *Anything. I can smell a nightgown. I can find Faith—? No. Yes. I can do anything for you, Rex. As long as—No. Yes. No.*

71

In the end, I lead them down to the river, right where the nightgown had been, and where I had dug for bones beneath the moonlit water. "Goddamn, that's a smart dog. I knew she could do it," crows Whitney.

"Doesn't give us much, though, does it?" said Rex. "Just tells us what we already knew. That Faith's nightgown was found down here by the river. They'll drag it today. They had to get a diver to come from Kingston." He pauses. "Goddamn it, they searched the house yesterday! They talked to everybody I work with. Jesus, Jesus, she's missing, and I have to put up with this shit!" He makes a wordless bursting noise, drags a hand down his face again, stretching it long and ugly the way I have seen him do when he wants to cry but won't. Whitney says nothing, looks at the ground. After a while he says, "Yeah man, they gave me the fifth degree too. Assholes."

He bends down. "Dinah, you idiot. Lookit. Here's your dog tag. It's got a little crown on it 'cause you're my princess, right, stupid? Heel now. Come on, girl."

The three of us go back, the men walking slowly. I try to keep up a good front, running with a stick, chasing a leaf. But I am thinking about domestication and compromises made for love. I have never been more aware of my wildness, of the awful tension at the middle of my happiness. It makes me hate them and makes them love me, but too much has passed and there is nothing for it except to run to exhaustion under the stars each night and die of a broken heart each time they go out.

That night, I returned to the hilltop. I found myself drawn, from the moment darkness fell. I hurried. There was some grand promise in the air. The moon had risen fat and yellow-bloody and was rapidly turning itself silver.

From far away I could hear them. The song was in full movement by the time I reached the rough circle of dogs, pushed my way in, settled my tail. I joined the random chant, meaningless syllables. Then the singing. My turn was coming.

Instinct is a hard-soft thing, like the bone in a tomcat's penis. When I reached the hard bone of instinct buried in my memory, I gripped it with my teeth, the teeth of my thinking, and shook it and worried it and gnawed it. I could feel the presence of another inside of me, filling me, forming itself to my form, some essential dogness that fashioned itself to my contours and pressed against my skin from within. The precise notes of my part of the song flowed from my throat like an endlessly moving current, a river from which I needn't drink, for I was the river. And as the pack sang its way back to when we were wolfish and wild and more hunter than hunted, my river diverged. The paw of my mind changed to palm, and I held grey-ivory bone. I gripped with my fingers. The bone was a club I could raise. My song river diverged again, and the bone became a stick that I could throw with a command to fetch. Frantic, I tried to sing my way back to the river, out of this tributary full of hairless feet and flattened muzzles and opposable thumbs. My voice rose in pitch, fighting against the current, struggling to return to the river. The other dogs fell silent and turned to me, their eyes flat with fear and hatred. Evey barked at me, but her words were incomprehensible. She barked again, and then all the dogs barked, leaping to their feet.

Shaking, I tried to explain, but could speak only nonsense. I fled down the hill, stumbling and sliding into a night world gone suddenly blank and threatening. I could hear them behind me, and—forgive me—I picked up a stone and hurled it. Someone yelped. I turned and faced the pack. The metal tags on their collars—rabies and distemper shots, license, I belong to—were tin stars in the night. I raised my arm again, fist around another stone, and they shrank back, already in retreat.

Cold and heart-rushed, I arrived at my door. I slid my fingers along the top of the door frame, searching for the hidden spare key. My fingertips touched cold metal. With the key in the lock, I turned to look into the neighbour's yard. I whistled for Dinah, Whitney's German shepherd cross. I whistled and called and clapped my hands twice, our signal. I whistled and called and clapped again. A light went on in Whitney's house, and I turned the key in the lock.

Stepping through the door, I heard Rex call out, "Faith? Is it you?" I said nothing, letting him slip back into his dream. Give him a chance, maybe, for the first few minutes, maybe, to decide it was a dream. I had learned to wait, in my dogness, and so I lay motionless and silent on the cool kitchen floor until the shadows around me collected themselves into the cold domestic shapes of fridge and stove, countertop and table. Then I went to him, where he was warm in our tousled bed, and slipped between the sheets. I curled into the curve of his reaching arms, pressing hard into him with my haunches.

I Am a Rich Man

I am shaving in front of the bathroom mirror. I am thinking of what it is like to become a rich man.

Beside me, my three-year-old son shaves along: he is using a plastic razor that he mows through the foam on his smooth skin, drawing the razor horizontally across the space between his nose and his upper lip. He has the body of a fat woman. When he runs from the bathroom, I am awed by his beauty.

It's odd, turning into a rich man, because it's coming late in life, and there are some things about it that I didn't anticipate. For example, I expected to be smarter about some things, like why people we've known for years say, "We'll have to have you and your family over," after they've come for dinner at our new house, when it turns out what they mean is "We will never invite you over, and we may never call again." I didn't expect that.

You wouldn't believe some of the gossip. A good friend my wife hadn't seen for a while came over, and when leaving said, "Well, I guess you haven't changed."

My wife said, "Changed in what way?"

"You know, become … uh …"

"Morally bankrupt?" my wife provided.

The friend laughed, but the look on her face first, according to my wife, was embarrassment because my wife had nailed it. So my wife laughed too, so as not to embarrass her further.

"Well, next time you come over," she said, "I won't bother to remove my baby seal fur slippers."

They're still friends.

My wife, who is very smart, could probably tell you five different reasons why I'm right when I say that "We must have you over" means never, never, never.

"Healthy shame," is the kind of thing she says. The thought-you-might-have-become-morally-bankrupt friend was embarrassed by healthy shame.

The difference between my wife and me is that she can tell you why. I can just tell you what.

She would likely be able to tell me why, for example, I felt ill yesterday afternoon. I had been out for lunch with my boss, a guy I like well enough to go for lunch with. We'd gone to this excellent sushi place about halfway down the block from where we work. And while we were having lunch, a woman I would have called a friend only a month before she came in, came in.

She came into the restaurant, and a smile arrived on my face of its own accord. Excited to see her, I started to rise from my chair, and my mouth opened to call her.

But before anything could come out of me—and I'm lucky it happened this way, I know—she hit me with a glare so hard I felt it. I froze in a zed shape, my butt hovering above the seat.

I had forgotten that she now hates me.

I had forgotten! I am supposed to hate her too, but I forgot! I forgot. She hates me in the way that includes giving me a crazy, dirty-eyed glare when she sees me in a restaurant, so I have to hate her back, I guess.

This former friend of mine is very fat, and the cut-eyed look did nothing for her. Her eyes are already small and piggy because of her face fat, and her nose has the shape that can only be called Fat Person Nose.

These are the kinds of thoughts you have about a person when you hate them. I'm catching on. But when she was my friend, I thought she was beautiful. Or rather, I considered her elegant.

"Friend of yours?" my boss said and turned his head. He came around rather quickly, and in fact he only said, "Friend of yo—" and then stopped. I realized my mouth was kind of spread across my face, because he looked at me with some alarm. "Something wrong?" he asked.

"Former client," I lied.

In our business, there are former clients, and it's just part of the job that sometimes you don't win the suit. But this friend, she had been a *friend*, not just a client. A friend first.

My bowels seemed to be going all watery, but I thought it would be safer to stay at the table and hang on than to try to get to the restroom.

I felt ashamed. Not of the gut ache, but of the smile, the one that had leapt to my face when I saw her. I feel ashamed when I admit this.

Once, when I was about seven, I let our family dog off his leash on our way to the park. I was forbidden to release him until we were in the park, but Seamus, a sheltie, was so eager that I unhooked the leash from his collar while we were across the street from the park, and the minute I let him go he ran out straight into the path of an oncoming streetcar.

There was no warning cry or squeal of breaks. The streetcar was just coming to its stop. Seamus ran right under the terrifying track-grooved iron wheels and disappeared.

I stood immobile while the waiting passengers boarded and the streetcar pulled away from the concrete island, stuck in its fixed lines. Where the streetcar had been, Seamus lay on his side.

People heading toward the stop rushed when they saw him. Their noises sounded all the same: one after another, they went *aaaw, aaaw, aaaw*, like the sound of geese from a long way off. A few of them knelt around Seamus. A sheltie is a long-haired dog whose fancy coat gives it the appearance of being permanently in black tie. Seamus lay there, with his neat white paws crossed one over the other, and his long-haired, precisely patterned coat spread around him like a dressing gown. More people knelt down close to him, stroking his thick coat, and then a few more, and then I couldn't see him anymore.

When I got home, I told my mother and I swear it felt like the truth. I told my mother Seamus had run away and would not come back when I called him. I had only called him inside my head, but I did not tell her that.

We went out together to search for him right away, my mother in a brown coat with two rows of buttons. She had snow boots on, but only with nylon stockings, nothing warm. A hat but no gloves. I tried to keep her hand warm with mine as she held it, pulling me along toward the park. I lied and told her that Seamus and I had taken the down-the-block-past-the-gas-station route, and so we never went past the streetcar stop at all.

"He'll come back, honey. Seamus is a smart dog and knows his way home." I knew she was wrong.

I was red eyed and sniffling at dinner, and my mother told my father what had happened to me, in a tone that mothers use to give direction of an emotional nature to the fathers of their children.

I know this tone because my wife uses it on me. It's a broad vocal wink, indicating how she wants me to react to something. For example, last week she greeted me with "Look, honey. Gabriel made you a Happy Birthday." Her eyes were very wide and a bit wild looking, as was the smile stretching her mouth. She looked like she was acting in a silent movie.

In the living room, every leaf had been stripped from every plant: rubber trees, *Ficus benjamina*, amaryllis and narcissus, half a dozen flowering hibiscus, bougainvillea. It's my wife who knows the names of them. I secretly think *rhubarb* whenever I look at any one of them.

The leaves and flowers were roughly laid out on the floor, spread carefully over as much area as possible. A small, mostly deflated balloon rested in the centre, with a weird little pucker on its side.

My son was vibrating with excitement, his smile stretching his neck and jaw as though he had been stricken with rictus. "Pursize!" he finally exploded, when he could stand it no more, and he grinned so hard his clenched teeth made the tendons in his neck tent out.

It wasn't my birthday, or anyone's.

"Thank you!" I exclaimed, and my wife … *beamed*, is the word. Her face actually beamed light at me.

When my mother told my father at the dinner table that Seamus had gotten away from me at the park, my father said, "Oh?" with a kind of jiggle to his head, straightened his shoulders, and launched into a story of how he had been told, as a child, that his mother had died in hospital and he had not been allowed to see her or attend her funeral. While he talked, he kept his eyes on his fork, knife, and plate. He ate steadily. The look on his face remained conversational.

I swear that in the time it took him to tell the story, I forgot about Seamus, stunned by my father's ability to remain expressionless as he cut, stabbed, bit, chewed, and swallowed.

After dinner we played Chinese checkers.

All this came back to me while I sat at the restaurant table with my boss, gripping the table edge.

"Yeah," my bossing was saying. "Yeah, beentheredonethat," smirking with his mouth and his eyes at the same time. I concentrated on my chopsticks, as though it took me more effort than it really did to use them. As if I had never eaten sushi with my boss before. And that was it. That's why I like the guy enough to go out for lunch with him.

When they were leaving the restaurant, that woman and the person she was with, I kept my face turned toward my boss's and laughed right on time at the joke he'd been telling.

When she had decided to hate me, it felt like it came from out of the blue: a message on my voicemail so vicious I barely recognized her voice.

I listened to it firing me, played it twice, and then, for some reason, erased it. Closed the file. Never called back. Sent no invoice. Admin automatically sent her a birthday card, which she mailed back to the office cut into pieces and X'd all over in black marker.

But whatever had landed on me when my friend walked in had hit like a meteorite on the dinosaurs. See? I called her *my friend* again. She is my friend. I see her and I think *friend* and have to be reminded by her Fat Person Squint that she hates me now.

When we were friends, I never called her fat, even in my mind. When we met, her father had been in the hospital, dying.

80

When it was time to plan the funeral, I went with her. I wanted to. It felt good; it felt right. I could help.

Did I stop helping? Did she stop needing my help?

I talked to my wife about it, and she listened, and she was helpful. But you know, she's my wife, not my best friend. Those people who say, "I married my best friend"? Well, what are they going to do in the event of a divorce? Lose everybody all at once?

Besides, my wife is different with her friends than I am with mine: She doesn't have more friends than I do, but they all seem like the type who would dispose of a body in the middle of the night with no questions asked, if my wife asked them to. She could show up at their door in the night and the rain with a shovel in one hand, and most of her friends would just nod and say, "I'll get a tarp." My friends are work guys or club guys or other board members. I like them. They like me. But no dispose-of-the-body stuff.

Except, I guess, for her: Fatty. She would have disposed of a body with me. I think. And she would have cried when I did not cry. And then she would have wanted me to hug her and maybe to kiss her.

And maybe we just weren't going to stay friends.

God, I hope I never have to date again.

When I got home that night, my little boy ran the length of our long living room, unimpeded by potted trees (my wife ditched them), and threw himself at me so hard that I rocked backward with him and landed beneath his laughing, wriggling self. I had just enough time to register that his face was smeared with something bright red. He'd either gotten into my wife's lipstick or eaten a clown. My wife came around the corner racing after the boy, and her lipstick looked like a madwoman had applied it too. She laughed at my boy and me writhing on the floor. The handle of my briefcase was still in my gloved hand. I was wearing a pair of John Lobb loafers that make my feet look longer than they really are, and for a moment I felt like a clown being pinned by another clown. I laughed so hard tears came to my eyes. I sat up and kept laughing and crying and kept on crying and had to drop my head. The crying wouldn't stop. Not right away.

"What's the matter?" my wife asked, squatting beside me and looking hard into my face in the calm way she has.

"There, there," my little boy said, switching gears, patting my back. It came out *dare, dare.*

"I had a dog named Seamus when I was seven, and he got hit by a streetcar when I was out walking him," I blubbed.

My wife is patient and understanding and good in a crisis. She is kind. I love her like my own heart. But she is my wife.

"Well what were your parents doing letting a seven-year-old walk a dog in the city anyway, for goodness sake?" she asked. "People shouldn't be allowed to have a pet until they're thirty years old. My stars, how stupid! It's like letting a seven-year-old become a parent. What were they thinking of? We wouldn't get a baby for a baby, would we, my baby?"

This last part she said while scooping our son up off the floor and mashing her face into his stomach. He laughed, and she did it again.

"You don't let a baby have a baby do ya baby?" she asked him, shaking her head and pressing it into his body. "Dooya baby, dooya baby, dooya baby?" Our son screamed with laughter.

When my wife finally put him down, with a final kiss to his belly, he pressed himself to me and said, "Feel my cheek." He pronounced it *sheik*.

I felt it.

"Soft," I said.

"Smooth," he corrected me.

I squeezed him. He ground his cheek into my after-work stubble.

My wife handed me a dried leaf from one of the plants.

I am a rich man. I am a rich man.

My Baptism

My baptism was quite special. I wore a red velvet dress. It was a miracle of dress engineering. It was a strapless thing that defied gravity. It had a shawl collar that orbited my shoulders like the rings of Saturn. It was a great dress. Annie Lennox wore the same dress in the video for "Money Can't Buy It." I lent it to her for the video. At my baptism, I waded into the River of Babylon up to my armpits. The River of Babylon. Jesus did my baptism himself. He spread his hand over my face and pushed a little so that I would fall backward into the water. I pushed back. He pushed harder 'cause he was getting annoyed. Dirty Jesus. Slow to anger, my eye. I let my knees break and went under the water. I held my nose with one hand. Jesus was supposed to spot me. I guess I pissed him off. He didn't keep his hand under my back. I guess I was supposed to come up on my own all spitting and crying and all and saying how great it was and everything. I did a scissor kick and got away. Jesus said Hey, but someone else, maybe Peter or somebody like that, said Let her go man. The apostles all look like hippies, exactly the way they did in the movie *Jesus Christ Superstar.* They didn't even put on makeup or costumes to do that movie, they just played themselves. That's what Norman Jewison said, Just be yourselves. Some of them didn't even wash their faces 'cause they said that it wasn't authentic, that they were dirty a lot when they were hanging out with Jesus, and that it would be more authentic if they were a bit dirty. Most of them brushed their teeth though because a lot of them were trying to make out with the Alvin Ailey dancer girls, and they found out pretty quick that Alvin Ailey dancer girls don't want to neck with apostles with bad breath, even if they are real apostles. Of course, this was long before I met Jesus or any of them, because that movie was made in 1973 and I was baptised in the eighties. I didn't really know Annie Lennox, she just asked to borrow my dress. She saw it at the baptism. She was dating one of the apostles. I wanted to say hi when I spotted her in the crowd, and that's when Jesus shoved my head under the water. It was like being in the pool with all the little kids shoving and pushing and jumping on each other. Some of the apostles had pool noodles. I started going down the river pretty fast. The River of Babylon has an undertow. The thing is, Jesus grabbed at the hem of my dress to keep me from getting away, but the dress sort of just got longer and longer, so even though I got farther and farther away, Jesus was still holding on to the hem of my dress, and some of the apostles started to laugh. Jesus tried to kind of throw the dress at me, but it was really long, like about ten yards long by then and really heavy 'cause it was soaking wet and velvet, and the dress and I were heading downstream, so it was dumb like when you throw a wadded up piece of paper really hard and it doesn't go anywhere 'cause it's still paper even if you squeezed it into a ball shape. I sort of laughed 'cause Jesus looked so mad. And the apostles on the shore of the River of Babylon started laughing, and Jesus turned around and started yelling at them, and he jumped up and down a bit 'cause he was so mad, and then he jumped up, and when he came down he landed on a rock wrong and slipped and got a soaker, and he tried to kind of laugh it off and act like it was cool, but it wasn't, and he was getting madder, and you could tell he thought it was all my fault, him looking bad and all. And he squinted at me floating down the river and sort of shook his fist like I'm gonna get you, like it was supposed to be funny but you could tell that it wasn't really a joke, he really was mad. He used the hem of my red dress to wipe his face off and tried to throw it at me again, but you know, it was just getting longer and longer, and he was a bit tangled up in the dress. I was getting farther and farther away as I did the Ophelia down the Babylon, sorry for mixing my references there, and soon Jesus was a tiny, mad speck. The River of Babylon goes around a little bend right near where we were doing the baptism, so when I got around the corner, I kicked over to the shore and hauled myself up it and started to wring out my dress. Pretty soon, I've got this long coil of wound up red velvet 'cause I'm wringing it out a few inches at a time, then hauling some more out of the water and wringing that out, and there's like this velvet rope like you have at the theatre while you're waiting for the stars to get out of their limousines and come up the red carpet. I used to date John Malkovich, and we went to those movie things all the time, so I'm pretty used to it, and it's no big deal. But where I was on the shores of Babylon, the ground was all covered with little pine cones and cedar fingers turned brown and nice soft dirt and old juniper because the River of Babylon, as many of you know, starts in the Muskokas, and, as some of you don't know, my dad was the King of Ontario for a while, so we've got this castle or palace or whatever right on Lake Muskoka near Bracebridge, across from Frank Miller's house near Santa's Village. It's close to Bangor Lodge, and Santa and my dad and Premier Miller used to go golfing there. So I was getting a bit bugged 'cause my red velvet dress was getting dirty as I hauled it up the shores of the River of Babylon, and it was getting heavier and heavier, and it was so long, there was no end in sight, and it got snagged on some rocks or something, or so I thought, so I waded into the water and sure enough, there's Jesus hanging on to the hem of my dress by his teeth, twisting around like a steelhead snagged in some wild rice grass. What a putz. Let go, Jesus, let go, I said. I hauled on the dress and landed Jesus who started coughing and spitting, and I thought he was barfing 'cause his shoulders were heaving up and down, and I said Hey Jesus are you okay, and he got up on his hands and knees, and his hair was in his face and everything, but I could tell he was crying. Jesus is crying. Hey Jesus don't cry I say and pat him on the back a few times. But he's still crying so hard he can't say much except buh-buh-buh, which changes after a little bit to nuh-nuh-nuh and then unh-unh-unh, and then he says: I. Like. Your. Dress. Oh hey thanks Jesus, I say. I like your dress too. And he says No I really like your dress. A lot. And he stops crying and sort of looks at me all meaningful and all, and I say Well thanks again. It's a pretty great dress, for sure. And he keeps looking real meaningful at me, and I finally say Do you want to try it on? And he nods all enthusiastic and everything, and we stand up and swap. When we're swapping, I get a peek, and Jesus is not a big guy, but very buff, so I think he must get an A in gym class. Now the thing is, Jesus and I are not the same size, and the red dress was about ten yards long when I pulled myself out of the River of Babylon, but when Jesus puts it on, it fits perfectly and he looks pretty nice. I get to wear his outfit, which is like a white hemp tunic and a blue bathrobe. You've probably seen it in pictures. Also the sandals. So Jesus is standing there in the red dress, and I say You look nice,

Jesus. And he says So do you, Janette. And he turns around and heads up toward the road that leads around the bay to the marina. And I say Where you going? And he says The marina. And I say See you there, and I step out across the lake.

Feminine Protection

The suction created when Stephanie closes the door of the plane's miniature washroom makes her ears hurt. Normally, this would annoy her, but this time she's not feeling annoyed.

She is feeling something, though. Not happy—she's not a fool, and there is too much hormonal upheaval. But she's not feeling anything like what some of her friends have described, "My arms ached to hold a child, and I wept every time I saw a woman with a stroller." To this, Stephanie always found herself thinking, *Well, why didn't you have the baby, then?*

Should she have cancelled her flight? What could she have said in explanation? There is no way for Stephanie to get out of this trip home or to truly be part of it. In a few hours, someone is going to ask, "How are you?" and she won't be able to answer. Not honestly, anyway. It's as though the only acceptable answer to that question for a person in her position is tears, remorse, rended garments, gnashing of teeth, pulling of hair, etc. "My arms ached to hold a child, and I wept every time I saw a woman with a stroller."

It's not acceptable for her to say, "Fine" or "Great!" or "Glad I'm not pregnant!"

The abortion itself, and the care she received before, after, and during from the clinic staff, had been impeccable: respectful, intelligent, kind. The procedure itself was uncomfortable, no question. Like having a tooth pulled, maybe an impacted tooth, with your feet in stirrups, naked from the waist down, flat on your back and knees apart. Really, more like a very lengthy Pap test. But with nitrous oxide. Eminently survivable.

After a minute, from behind her medical mask, the doctor had said, "You're not pregnant."

Stephanie had wanted to reply, "Wheeeee!" But even that would have been a stifle. The thing she really wanted to say was, "My name is Jane, and I am Not Pregnant!"

It was that old beer commercial. The one with the scruppy cute guy in a Scarborough dinner jacket, standing in front of a gigantic waving flag, ranting about being named Joe and being Canadian. Stephanie saw herself, for a moment, standing there wearing a—what do you call it—a hospital gown, with her arms stretched out, shouting, "I may not wear a toque or play hockey, but I can get a free abortion on demand! My name is Jane, and I am Canadian!"

Giddy from the nitrous oxide and relief, she'd settled for saying to everyone in the clinic in general, "I hope you all get the Order of Canada."

And from that moment, she'd been checking: Did she really mean it? Was this really guilt-free? Her stomach, her conscience, her heart, her gag reflex all said yes. So what was making her feel … what the heck was it, anyway?

The remnants of a guilt-free abortion are the same as those of the regrettable other kind, and so none of the flushable details will be described here. Stephanie handles the disposable cotton and paper products of abortion aftercare with the same detachment she has been handling her other feminine protection with since she was thirteen.

But it is different. She makes a speedy scrutiny of the gore on the surface of the pad, like she's speed reading tea leaves, checking for Rorschach evidence of regret or shame or worse. She knows herself pretty well, and so is aware that she could be drowned by these feelings. She just doesn't have them. In her twenties, when her friends were having abortions resulting from spottily applied birth control methods, Stephanie had almost felt left out.

She feels weird. Must be the turbulence.

Steph examines her reflection in the mirror. Thinking ahead to the next airport, the short drive, the arrival home, she imagines telling someone—a sister, a cousin—about the abortion and tries out a look of shame. The mirror shows her in a strangely familiar pose, and she realizes she reminds herself of the nuns in *The Sound of Music* when they show their Mother Superior the distributor cap they had eviscerated from the car of the nasty Nazis.

What she says to herself is, "How come I'm not crying?"

No answer.

"Would it feel different for someone who feels guilty?" Stephanie wonders, and wonders again why someone would do it if they did feel guilty about it. It's almost as if you're supposed to feel guilty, as though, even though it's available, and it's free, you have to hate yourself for doing it, or you're somehow … something. The answer won't let itself form in her head, so she leans against the cool tile of the wall and closes her eyes. "As though, if you do it, and you don't feel guilty about it, then you're a stupid loser just like the stupid losers you've spent all that time fighting for abortion rights for." Fuck it. What about just having an abortion because you didn't mean to get pregnant? Like, is it pro-choice, or is it pro-you-deserve-an-abortion-because-you're-dumb-or-poor-but-I-wouldn't-personally-get-one-myself?

93

She washes her hands in the tiny stainless steel sink, then takes her travel toothbrush and toothpaste from her bag. The toothpaste is pink, a new kind for sensitive teeth, and the gob that falls from the brush into the little basin lands in an unfortunately fetal shape.

Not a human fetus, necessarily. It looks as much like the evolutionarily obsolete vermiform appendix as it does an infant. She knows from biology that the embryos of all creatures resemble each other alarmingly in the early days of development: fish, elephant, boy. She knows it evolves, in utero, from blob to baby, and for her this is enough. A fertilized egg splits itself in two, and from there the microcosmic evolution is as strange and marvellous as the Darwinian kind. If people can accept blobhood to babyhood, why can't they accept the grander, external, visible, gapped-record kind of evolution as some miracle? Or as working in mysterious ways?

When Stephanie emerges from the airplane into the flexible tunnel that connects it to the airport, the landscape she sees through the window is disorientingly, maddeningly familiar. It is thoroughly unlike the landscape surrounding the airport from which she took off short hours ago, and so it seems that crossing half the country is like crossing a major city on public transit. She feels like she ought to be in the same place.

Clearly, she is not: there is her mother, standing near the terminal's baggage conveyor belt, waving and smiling, and smiling and waving. She looks pretty, and has taken care to do so. Stephanie recognizes this as one of the ways her mother tells her she loves her. She takes care with her appearance, the same way Stephanie does when she puts on mascara to have coffee with a friend.

They hug, pressing close to each other's bodies. Their heights, now almost identical, allow them to rest their heads on each other's shoulders, the way two horses will rest standing in a field.

Stephanie loves her mother. She knows she was a fetus inside this woman's uterus.

"My dove," says her mother, kissing her.

What Stephanie feels is tired. There had been local anaesthetic with the abortion and nitrous oxide. She'd had to fast the night before. She had worked a full day immediately following. She had rushed from work to the airport and had eaten nothing on the flight. Now is the time that she feels like crying.

"You look tired," her mother says, squinting at Stephanie.

"You look tired" does not mean "Let me take your suitcase" or "I'll drive"; it's code for "It wouldn't hurt you to put on a little make up." But because Stephanie is tired, she pretends to take it literally, as an out, and says, "I had to get up early for the flight," turning to the baggage conveyor.

"There's my suitcase," reaching past her mom and heaving it over the lip of the conveyor belt.

"Here, you drive," says her mom when they are in the parking lot, digging her keys from her purse.

Stephanie puts the suitcase in the trunk, gets into the driver's seat. Automatically, she reaches underneath to adjust the distance from the pedals and remembers she doesn't need to. Then she pauses, with the tip of the key touching, but not in, the ignition.

She is not so much remembering as allowing a certain memory to rise to the surface. An image, always there, just below the ice, visible, and shadowy sometimes, but sometimes dazzlingly clear: a moment, years ago, just before she left home. A half-hearted suicide attempt, some nonsense with a utility knife: horizontal, not up-and-down. Even she didn't take it seriously, knowing even then that horizontal meant you wanted to tell someone you were suffering, but not that you wanted to die. So she goes to her parents' room, where her mother snores softly in the dark. Her father, as usual, has fallen asleep in the reclining chair in his den with the TV still on. Stephanie usually turns it off as she heads to her own room. She knows he is happily deeply asleep, covered by an afghan, content until morning. She leaves the TV on.

In her parents' room, at her mother's side of the bed, she pauses a long moment, considering her options, but they are few. Her heart is beating too fast, and her breathing is making her feel light headed, and aren't you supposed to wake up your mom when you are afraid?

"Mom," she whispers, bending low, "Mom. Can you get up please? I just tried to commit suicide, and I need you to take me to the hospital."

Without looking at Stephanie, her mom struggles out from the covers, pulls slacks on under her nightgown. She is looking for a bra, and Stephanie gets her one from the dresser drawer, turns her back so her mom can dress.

In the driveway, her mother gets the key into the car door and gets in behind the wheel, but is flummoxed after that. She can't seem to get the key into the ignition.

"I don't think I can drive. Can you?" Her mom looks down as she says it, not looking at Stephanie, just down and forward.

By the time Stephanie is in the driver's seat thinking, *I'm in the driver's seat*, the truth has settled down inside of her like a drink of Alka-Seltzer: she actually feels good all of a sudden. They drive to a Dairy Queen, eat chocolate dip cones in silence, and go back home. The band-aid on her wrist has soaked up what little blood there was.

Now, in the airport parking lot, Stephanie starts the car, wondering if her mother has to push that memory down each time she gets in to drive, the way Stephanie does.

"Your cousin Monique will be there," she tells Stephanie.

"Really?" asks Stephanie. "I haven't seen her since her wedding."

"She just had a miscarriage." Her mother's voice is whispery, full of something—maybe reverence, maybe the self-conscious honour of being the first one to deliver terrible news.

"Really?" asks Stephanie.

She says it blithely, conversationally, fake-neutrally, but looks out the corner of her eye to catch her mother's response, which does not disappoint: her mother whips her head about, looks hard at Stephanie to see if she's being "saucy," frowns, and turns away.

Stephanie looks ahead, driving, says nothing.

"Stephanie," says her mother.

"What?"

"Well."

"What?"

"Give your head a shake."

Stephanie does, and her mom looks away, trumped.

After a while, her mom says, "Take a minute to say something nice to her."

"Yeah? Like what?" asks Stephanie, slowing to take the off-ramp.

"Just be kind. It's tragic."

"Ah," says Stephanie. And then, "Doesn't she already have a kid?"

"Two," says her mother.

"Then she can probably have another, right?"

"Steph-a-nie!" With the look again.

97

"But it's true, right? She can have another baby. Women get pregnant after them, you know. It happens all the time."

"Oh Stephanie." But her mother is logically cornered, and the conversation stops as they pull into the driveway.

What's not going to happen next is anyone taking care of Stephanie and her scraped-out uterus.

Many people are in the house, awaiting her arrival, come for the Easter long, long weekend. Good Friday and Easter Monday, and the Holy Saturday and Sunday in between. Cousins and aunts have travelled long and short distances by car—none from as far away as Stephanie has, but that was her choice.

Monique, the other recently non-pregnant woman in the house, stumbles up to Stephanie, special and red nosed, secure in the knowledge that her tragedy has been imparted and absorbed.

Stephanie hugs her wordlessly, patting her back, which Monique accepts with dignity before allowing herself to be repositioned on the sofa beside some other female family members, who close in around her protectively.

In her old bedroom, Stephanie is slightly surprised to find a sleeping child on the bed. Most of the kids—the children of Stephanie's siblings and cousins—are old enough to be downstairs in the rec room in the care of the dads. Steph can hear them at the ping pong table, her father bellowing fake colour commentary to spur the game on and keep the youngsters in a state of frenzied excitement.

This sleeping toddler must be one of Monique's. It's a pretty kid, clearly a boy from the clothes, with the preposterous cheeks and pursed cherry lips of his age. Stephanie knows his features will, in time, emerge from their sheath of fat and become the square chin and hard angles that every face in the family carries. He will be like the sparkling-edged figures that emerge out of blocks of sculpted ice as they begin to melt, ignoring the carver's intention and becoming something else.

She leaves her suitcase packed and tiptoes out so as not to wake the peaceful child.

In the kitchen, Stephanie dodges the female bodies that shuffle rapidly between counter, fridge, table, sink as though they were on an assembly line, instead of in her mother's ordinary kitchen. They are preparing the huge family breakfast for the next day, the one that will be served when they get back from Easter Mass, and they are banking effort against the time when they will sit down and relax and eat and laugh, before getting down to the business of preparing dinner.

Stephanie knows the routine and knows her place in it. Her fatigue from the flight and the night and day before does not disappear; it's just not that different from the tiredness most of the people in the kitchen probably also feel. She busies herself forming risen dough into chubby lengths, to be spread with butter and cinnamon and sugar before baking.

The aunts, the cousins, they say hello, they hug with floury hands. Stephanie has been living away from home a long time—six years—but her decision to leave in the first place was such a faux pas that they still politely refrain from mentioning it.

Monique is semi-invalided on the sofa in the living room, so the aunts bring her tea and date squares. From the kitchen, Stephanie watches her from the corner of one eye, noting the perfect-triangle composition of grieving almost-mother, flanked by large aunts: one a nun, the other, a mother of twelve surviving children, is likely the veteran of several miscarriages herself.

That aunt goes to see about an escalating wail snaking up from the basement, and the nun aunt remains, patting Monique, but stealing glances at a newspaper unfolded to the sports section, resting on the ottoman beneath Monique's legs.

Stephanie exits the kitchen, accepting sweet hugs from fat arms as she threads her way out. She fills in for the departed aunt, taking up the position like a good left defence at the line change.

The nun aunt gives her a smile but says nothing, for she is pressing Monique's head to her shoulder. Monique's eyes are shut, and she breathes with a soft growl.

"We put brandy in her tea," says the aunt to Stephanie.

Stephanie has not been offered any of the brandy or sherry traditional to this day and this gathering, much less the beer certain to be found in quantity in the basement. The dads of the air-hockey playing kids will be drinking it, taking it out of the basement fridge and offering it around like wine at the Last Supper.

It's like she's still a kid, and even though she is older than the sleeping Monique, she knows her status is not taken seriously. Her bed will be given to grown-ups—likely Monique and her Anglo husband. It won't surprise her if she is relegated to the card table that will crouch at the end of the big table to make room for kids at dinnertime.

Monique is conferred with childbearing, clearly. But what about the nun?

They are silent, the two childless women and the sleeping mother between them. Which is fine with Stephanie. She has always felt a certain connection to the nun and assumes that this feeling is reciprocated. Stephanie waits, not wanting to interrupt her aunt, who has leaned forward to pull the sports page out from

Monique's sleep- or brandy-heavy legs, then mentions to her, "I don't believe in God."

"That's all right," says the nun without hesitation, nodding slightly several times. She draws Stephanie's eyes to her own and gazes there with interest. "That's all right," she repeats, and then, with effort, drags her gaze back to the sports page. "You don't have to." For a brief, breath-clenched second, Stephanie waits for the aunt to say, "He believes in you." But she doesn't, God bless her.

Some kind of peace descends upon Stephanie, and she finds she is ravenous. When she rises to go toward the kitchen, she hears the little boy on her bed cry out, his alarm at waking in an unfamiliar place apparent in his wordless voice.

She goes to him where he sits on his blanket as though it were a raft and he the stranded castaway, and gathers his limbs into hers. To her surprise, he stops crying and falls back into sleep almost immediately.

"That's all right," she murmurs to him, her lips brushing the damp curls of his head. After a moment, she lowers him back onto the bed. One hand drops heavily onto the mattress, and the child's fingers shoot out reflexively before drifting slowly downward to alight on the blanket—the releasing of marionette strings by a puppeteer who has slipped drunkenly under the stage.

The hallway from her room to the kitchen seems very short, and the light and warmth from it, very strong. They are gathered there now: all the feminine protection she could hope for. They are all holding glasses of sherry, toasting each other on having finished their preparations for the next day.

The nun aunt, now with the rest of them in the kitchen, makes sure that Stephanie's glass comes from her hand. The two of them tap the delicate rims of the sherry glasses together. In Stephanie's ear, it rings and rings, and in spite of its smallness against the kitchen din, it sounds like distant cheering.

Invisible Friends

The children lie facedown, arms flung up and out above their heads. The boy's mattress is directly on the floor, the lower half of his body still on it, his naked torso in a pool of his own pyjamas. The girl is half-on, half-off her own mattress, upper body tangled in the bedclothes, bare feet showing dirty soles, edged pink. Her head is twisted sideways, mouth pressed open to the floor in a last secret whispered or a final scream.

"It looks like a bloodless massacre," the woman says, bending slightly to switch on the plug-in nightlight.

"Come on," says the man, "don't even say stuff like that."

"Like what?"

"Like 'bloodless massacre.' They're our kids, not Bonnie and Clyde."

"The Clutters. I was thinking of the Clutters, not Bonnie and Clyde."

"Who are the Clutters?"

"Were. They're that family from *In Cold Blood*."

"For God's sake."

He's used to it, Hugh is, but tired of it at the same time. So is Liz, but she can't seem to stop it.

It has been going on since way before she had kids. Okay, for her whole life. Stuff just coming in like visits from some invisible friends. Although they're not always friendly. And not invisible. To her.

But no psychic vision shit, thankfully. Nothing that ever came true. So she had never actually opened the fridge and found a woman's hand wearing her mother's wedding ring, centred on a plate between a Tupperware container and a carton of milk.

That one had been a bit of a bugger, though, accompanied as it had been by a man's voice commanding, "Get out!" as she gripped the handle of the refrigerator, elbow bent in the air like a carpenter's square. Just what is the point of smoking pot if this is what's going to happen?

Since she did not for a second believe that there was some-body inside her head telling her to axe murder her parents, she swore that would be the last time she got high by herself instead of going to church.

But if she was going to be honest, the pot wasn't to blame. It wasn't the first time she had heard a voice talking to her when no one was there. So she didn't take it personally or anything. Just figured "Get out!" was some kind of internal advice, delivered—alarmingly, granted—by a disembodied, unknown male voice. And the hand-in-the-fridge thing had maybe been a bit over the top. But it was okay advice, anyway.

She had been about seventeen at the time. She'd gotten right into the car and driven around until her parents got home from church. She left home within the year. A lucky scholarship and a university two provinces away. Quite a lot less pot smoking, as it made it hard to study, but no end to the little visits by the invisible friends.

When she had been very small, she just figured it was normal. Or part of normal. One from when she was very little: in the kitchen with her mother and the aunts, the older kids running around in another part of the house, her aunts outlined by colour as they moved around the kitchen, rays of colour detaching themselves

104

from the grownups, shifting, decomposing and recomposing, returning in different combinations. Interesting to the point of fascinating while she gummed Cheerios in her high chair, but not something to talk about because, frankly, at her age, rainbows around your aunties, a man on TV who lands on the moon, pooing and peeing at the same time, your own sneeze, and a dancing dog who barks bullets, balloons, streamers, and confetti, could all be considered equally weird, as everything was for the first time, and besides, she couldn't talk yet.

Another one, a little after that, older now, in elementary school: a mean teacher who for a moment was a little less threatening because the ugly dwarf mummy hiding inside her tummy was not only thrashing its arms and legs, making its bandages come undone, but also making the same ugly faces that the yelly teacher was, at the same time she was.

Not exactly what could be called invisible friends. She never felt lonely and never ever alone. But they weren't something you talked about because other people would think you were crazy.

Like that psychology major in first year university telling her that it was a symptom of depression. Huh. Depression, eh? She didn't feel depressed.

She and the psych major had been heading to a party in the dark down a back road, Liz driving, the cute psych major on the passenger's side, and Liz remarked, "Don't you ever expect to come around a corner like this and find, like, a zombie hunched over somebody in the middle of the road, gobbling them up?"

The psych major responded, "Do you?" leaning in and breathing it on her neck like it was dirty talk. "Are you unstable? Are you psychopathological? Nymphomaniacal?" He asked, trying to sound all psych major-y and sexy at the same time. Liz concentrated on driving.

"Are you abnormal? Are you insane? Are you crazy? A freak?" He took her hand off the steering wheel, put it in his lap: "Do you want to gobble me up?" he asked, still in that phase where he thought you had to trick the other person into doing it.

She swerved the car a little to avoid the not-there zombie and to get the psych major off her.

"Hey!" he protested, shifting back to his side of the car. "I thought you were coming on to me." Jesus! Was he sulking?

"You might be crazy. Clinically depressed, you know? Seeing stuff that's not there. Zombies."

That was the last time Liz said anything to anyone about the invisible friends. She'd slip up, of course. She couldn't help it.

Hugh just seemed to think it was her hearing or maybe her sense of humour. Like, as friends were leaving after a good visit, she might holler, "Now don't be a strangler! Come back soon!" Hugh would laugh because the first time he'd said, "Don't be a stranger," Liz looked alarmed and said, "Why would he be a strangler?" because she truly had never heard the expression before and had truly misheard him.

It became a running joke with them; Liz would confuse *strangler* and *stranger*, always laying it at the door of someone who would likely never, ever do anything creepy, much less go home to do some strangling.

But here was Hugh now, giving a soft but heart-felt sigh in response to her remark about the Clutters in the Capote book. That poor family: the bedridden mother with undiagnosed depression, the rancher dad, the boy with that odd name, Kenyon, and the girl—Dick Hickock thinking he might "bust her cherry" and Perry Smith shaming him out of it before shooting the girl in the back of the head.

"Maybe you're doing that, uh, whaddya call, magical thinking," says Hugh now, his arm around her waist tightening into a full hug. "Maybe you figure that if you say those things, they won't happen, is that it?" he asks, talking into her hair. "That you can keep it away by saying it out loud, is that it? If you make a joke of it?"

She shakes it off, still standing in the doorway of the kids' room, her face and eyes turned toward them where they are slumped on the carpet. She hadn't been a frightened kid, and her kids aren't the jumpy, timid sort either. It's the difference between knowing it's scary and being scared.

She watches for it in them, her kids. The oldest, her daughter, had gone through a phase where she seemed able to read Liz's mind—but then, you know what they say: kids notice everything. Like the time she'd said, after the grandparents had left, in the kindest, most admiring four-year-old voice she had, "Grandpa is just like Grandma's baby."

All innocence, but really, really true in a way that made Liz and Hugh laugh. The way Hugh's mother serves her husband first at dinner, makes sure he's the first one to get ice cream, giving him the biggest scoop, as if he were still a growing boy and the ice cream a treat for being a good one.

There was some truth in it, for sure. Liz had kind of been thinking the same thing, but in a much, much meaner way, like "Jesus Christ, what is she? His mommy?" That kind of thing.

She'd used it as an opportunity to be truthful with her daughter, to affirm the child's instincts and reality: "Yes, honey, Grandpa is like Grandma's baby."

Hugh elbowed her.

"Hey. Out of the mouths of babes ..." she said.

"Go on. You're only saying that because you agree with her."

"No!"

"Yeah. It's like when you say to me, 'you're really smart,' you generally mean that my opinion is the same as yours."

"You're so smart!"

"See?"

He hugs her again, or she notices his arm is pulling her closer. The kids are asleep, and his hand travels up from her waist, and he starts to play her ribs with his fingertips like they are a keyboard, edging upward, but when Liz brings her arm in close, trapping his hand against her body, he understands no.

Hugh stills, they both still to see if either will insist, then Hugh accepts it, lets it go. Part of the slow waltz of marriage, the dance steps taking days and weeks, and this is how time passes and how the years turn into the past.

Hugh withdraws his hand, kisses her on the face. He goes.

It's one of the many reasons they're still together.

That, and the fact that when he is near there is none of this shit with the invisible friends. She's not crazy, but it takes a certain amount of energy, having to choose, all the time, to monitor it. Hugh being part of things helps. Is it a good enough reason to love someone? That their presence keeps the bad things away? For Liz it is. Has been.

Until recently. Lately, she has found herself wanting to tell someone about the odd, corner-of-the-eye visions she lives with so lightly. Lately, that is, since she'd left the working world to stay home with the kids. But that was almost five years ago, since the first baby, the girl. She's been at home with them since.

Staying home has returned Liz to her own heavily populated childhood world. But now that she is the apparent adult, and these beautiful little children are so apparently separate people in a separate world, she is sharply aware of how spooky Kidland was. Is. As if she'd never really left it behind: the landscape has changed, as has the population, but it is still deeply familiar.

She spots a toy against the wall, the Incredible Hulk on a three-wheeled ATV, parked at an angle into the corner. Hulk starts to turn his thick head on his thick neck toward her, and she thinks *Don't* at him and he stops.

See? It's slipping. She's slipping. Don't talk to them, not even in your head. It's one of the rules.

She learned this the time she was on a chairlift, going up a mountain in Vermont, and that shitty thing came hunching out of the woods. Hairless and unclothed, it was bi-pedal and bilaterally symmetrical, mostly human shaped but lizard-ish, Creature-from-the-Black-Lagoon-ish, with a leathery hide and a face that looked right at her as she hung suspended in the metal swing of the chairlift, which had come to a stop the way chairlifts will, in mid-air, halfway up the hill—like, you know you're not supposed to be afraid, because somebody probably just dropped a ski pole while getting on, but Christ! You're not usually staring into the goat-eyes of some Black-Lagoon freak whose face armour is roughly in the shape of ski goggles, already.

She had only been able to stare back, but the question formed in her mind, not in the shape of words, not even in her mind's ear, and was apparently heard by the thing, anyway, because it answered, loudly, directly inside of her: "Because We can, shithead." Just like that, with an audible capitalization of the *W* on "We."

She had gotten the message. Don't ask. Or at least, don't talk to them. If you do, they'll talk back.

A few moments later, the lift restarting with a lurch, the chair drew her slowly past some graffiti spray-painted on the metal girders of one of the lift towers: "Chupacabra." As if she hadn't already gotten it, as if the thing had wanted to be sure.

Why not add "was here"!? she immediately thought, hysterically, the scene starting up again, the creature with its raised heels and fine-boned ankles—or maybe those were shins?—perched on the cables of the lift tower with a can of spray paint in its scaly hand, shaking the can like mad in the cold air, the nozzle clogged or something. She laughed to herself and the cables disappeared: now the chupacabra hovered in mid-air, stopped shaking the can to turn its face to her, and she felt suddenly afraid. But then the lift reached the top of the hill, where the air, thin and brittle, shattered both the vision and the feeling that came with it.

But. That was before kids.

Now, the invisible friends seemed to be getting closer, closing in. Landscape and weather deepening darker. Not sinister, exactly, or at least not exclusively. Like there had been a settling, a dimming down, of whatever brightness had fallen from the air with the kids at their births. As though, in leaving behind their infancies like clothing abandoned at the river's edge, the brown waters they dove into became their day sky, and above them, around them, surrounding everything, the light was muddy yellow, diffuse and rich with silt. River-bottom mud, sparks of mica and silica shooting up like stars, kicked up by their dives and drops.

And through this murk she can see her children, unclothed and clean, turn in the water, and with each twist they lengthen—the fat bellies melting, the torsos narrowing—becoming leggy, school-aged children, then leggier adolescents, stretching to the point of runway-model ridiculousness.

But of course, at the same time, she also just sees them as sleeping toddlers, on the floor, on their mattresses. Kids move around a lot in sleep, as if looking for something under the pillow or under the sheet, and then immobilize heavily, like bodies dumped at a construction site after a contract hit.

These two, right now, with their arms up as though raised in cagey fake surrender, just before drawing and gunning each other down at the same moment, they're just children in sleep, a brother and sister in the summer before school.

The boy twitches: a mouse in a sticky live trap. For the rest of their lives they will long for rest like this, the feeling of being slain by sleep. Through the day they have slain each other with laughter, shrieks of goading in toilety contests. The little one talks in his sleep, crying out perfectly articulated nonsense from the world of three without waking himself up, even though it's startlingly loud. He's a heavy sleeper.

Why does she see them this way, then? Aren't they happy? Isn't she happy? In the night, the night before this one, before this day of brown river water, the boy had burst into their bedroom, running in his sleep, if that were possible, pushed the covers aside and thrown himself on top of her, saying only, "I don't want to die," just once before falling back into sleep, before she could even say to him, "Shhh, shhh. You're not even awake."

What has she done to them? What horror has she brought into them? To give them life, to let them love it, and to be unable to tell them that they will never have to die?

"I'm sorry," she had wanted to whisper to him in the dark. And she was. But she couldn't say it. To do so would be to admit her mistake, a mistake there could be no undoing.

It's not a joke. It's deadly serious, and she knows it. She's always known, and maybe that's why she doesn't tell anyone.

Back and forth, back and forth. Kids asleep on the floor, light on in the bathroom, sound of brushing teeth from down the hall, Hugh getting ready for bed without her.

She's glad to be going back to work in the fall, when both kids will be in school, with the new all-day kindergarten. She's back in the same hospital, same ER. There is always a job for an ER nurse, and she has a rep for being absolutely unshakeable. Before she quit to stay home with the kids, she had been head of the trauma response units. Nothing scared her. Wonder why.

She could be crazy, but she's not.

Hugh kisses her on the way from the bathroom.

"Coming?" he asks.

She shakes her head no.

The Incredible Hulk shakes his head too; he doesn't turn away from the wall, but shakes his fat head, the triangular points of purple hair on the back of his green neck swing with the movement of it. Shit. That's not supposed to happen. Not with Hugh in the same room.

"Okay. Don't stay up too late," kissing her again, this time on the back of the neck. "Don't be a … "

"Strangler!" she finishes, putting her hands around an invisible neck and shaking it a bit to make Hugh laugh as he goes upstairs. She hears him tread on the seventh stair. It groans like an old dog in old-dog sleep.

Liz stays up late reading the newspaper. She doesn't watch TV. She scours the obits and trolls every section for stories about violence and weirdness and tragedy. Maybe Hugh is right: each rape or murder that does not happen to her or her family is one more bullet dodged. Or maybe she's slowly drawing these things into their lives, pulling horror in toward them on some kind of psychic tractor beam.

She should be crazy, but she's not.

Once, in emerg, there had been a highway collision that brought in a family of four in various states of brokenness. A face peeled down off the skull, legs twisted around so the feet faced backward, a complete disembowelment with lengths of chrome and plastic where the guts should have been, and the last family member—blond, solid: an angel-faced youngster—almost decapitated, the beautiful, unmarred face and head severed, attached to the neck by the barest of shreds. Dead dead dead.

Liz had taken the soft, full cheeks in her palms and positioned the child's head on a pillow, pressed the gore into place, straightening up. She combed the milkweed-soft hair with her fingers. The mother would not waken to see this; the father was already dead.

If ever, that was the time Liz expected the eyes to blink open, exposing blue stars. But nothing.

Sitting with the paper at the kitchen table, Liz is still.

Then she hears the muffled, familiar sound of the little boy's footfall above her head, in the kids' bedroom above. He has gotten himself up off the floor and is sleep-stomping into Hugh and Liz's room to roll himself up onto her side of the bed and curl there, as he does most nights, until either she or Hugh carries him back to his own bed without waking him. Sure enough, the silence the boy makes when he is hogging her side of the bed is loud overhead.

But then, for the second time in minutes, she hears the creak from the floor above that only comes when the threshold into the children's room is breached.

Smoothly, as if she has been waiting for this, just for this, she rises in one motion from the sofa, switching off a wall switch at the same time, and slides on sock soles to the kitchen drawer where she has been keeping the big-blade screwdriver.

She gets it from the back of the drawer, where she has always kept it.

Dead silent on the stairs, she stays to the outside edges of the risers, skipping the seventh stair entirely. Stays close to the wall when she reaches the top, turns into the children's open doorway with her shoulder still against the wall, the screwdriver ready.

She knows to step high over the threshold into the room. With her foot hovering, she checks with the Incredible Hulk, who is unmoving. She goes in.

So she is there when Hugh is still over the little girl, hunching with his face near hers. And Liz knows the force of the screwdriver into the base of his skull, right into the foramen magnum opening, will kill him instantly and with very little blood, and that the momentum of her kneeling down to do it will be all the force required because the point of entry is so strangely perfect—

Or not so strange—and he will simply go limp. So she must be ready to move—

"Mama?"

The room fills with starlight. The girl's eyelids almost close, almost close, close—and the starlight goes out.

Hugh finishes tucking the blankets around the girl, straightens her neck on the pillow so she won't get a kink.

He kisses the child high on the forehead, in her hair. Gets up. Tiptoes over to Liz, still in the doorway.

"Hey," says Liz in a whisper.

Silence silence.

"Did she wake up?" It's Liz who breaks it.

Hugh shakes his head, says, "Sometimes I just come in to see if she's okay. After Fatty there—" he jerks his head toward their room, where the little boy, not fat at all, but formerly the fattest baby either of them had ever seen—"after Fatty there rolls in for the night. He wakes me up."

"And then," he goes on, after a while, "I tuck her up, and I, I …"

Liz waits. She starts to think, *Don't tell me*, then she thinks to herself not to think that, and Hugh goes on talking.

"… because when I was a kid … some things happened to … my best friend. To him and his sister. That sounds like lying, but it's not. Their dad, or their stepdad. I don't know. It happened when I was there once, sleeping over. We were all three sleeping in their room, and."

She thinks, *Maybe there's stuff he's never told me.*

"There's stuff I've never told you, I guess," he continues. "I should. I never used to think about it, didn't even remember it for a while, but now I can't forget."

He notices what's in her hand.

"What are you doing with the screwdriver?" he whispers to Liz.

Liz wants to lean against the crooked doorjamb and laugh, but knows it would be too hard to explain to Hugh.

"Fixing things," she answers.

"Want help?"

"No. No, they're fixed."

They both stand there looking at the screwdriver in her hand.

Then Liz holds it out in front of her, by the blade, not the handle, like she's holding a rose by its stem. "For you," she says, holding it out to him. "Please. Take it. A token of my affliction."

Hugh puts the end of his long nose to the top of the screwdriver as though sniffing a flower, an iris or a daffodil. Nope, it's a rose: with his eyes on hers, he tilts his head, slowly, keeps tilting, tilts it until his mouth is parallel with the vertical handle of the screwdriver, then opens his lips with a quiet smack, square white teeth open too, so Liz knows to put the stem of the rose between them. He brings his head to centre, deadpan, not smiling, but with his eyes getting into it, his eyebrows waggling suggestively at her so Liz has to stifle what would be something between a guffaw and an unsexy snort. He cocks one eyebrow high, raises one arm up, bent elbowed like a flamenco dancer, and she admires his pirouette down the hall to their room. He's skinny, always will be, always was. She watches him go down the hall. He has no idea how good he looks, or how funny. He does another turn in the doorway of their bedroom, undoes the top button of his pyjama top, grimace-smiles at her from around the screwdriver blade, snaps his fingers like he thinks a flamenco dancer would do.

He will carry the little boy back to his bed in the room with

116

the sleeping girl, so he and Liz can lock their door and use the big bed. Or maybe they will look at the boy sleeping there and decide to leave him where he is and go downstairs to the carpet in the living room or maybe the pull-out couch in the basement. Lots of options. Anyway, it will work out all right.

Liz leaves herself behind, leaves her laughing self leaning against the doorjamb of the kids' room, leaves behind her self that was ready to kill, and goes after her husband, who holds for her a token of her affliction, into the bright dark.

Not *The Battleship Potemkin*

It's just a woman pushing a baby carriage. It's not *The Battleship Potemkin*. But because it's Jess pushing the baby carriage, she sees the two girls walking toward her on the sidewalk at the same time she sees the other little girl crossing the park with her mother, in split-screen.

On the sidewalk: two girls, seven or eight years old, premonitions of adolescence. Long-legs awkward with knobby knees. Shoulders and elbows bump together. Their smooth-haired heads tilt together, forming an arrow which points toward the park, pulling focus, drawing the eye to the action.

Jess pans to follow the arrow, focusing for a moment on the girl and her mother moving diagonally across the park. Then she cross-cuts to the girls on the sidewalk.

FIRST GIRL
Look, there's Veronica.

SECOND GIRL
(a little excited, maybe happy to see her?)
Yeah!

FIRST GIRL
(all one word)
Ihateher.

SECOND GIRL
Really?
(beat)
I mean, me too.

Jess sees their trajectories in a crane shot: they will intersect on the sidewalk directly in front of her, or rather, directly in front of the baby carriage.

In the park, the girl Veronica walks with her head down. She knows the girls on the sidewalk are there, seeing her. She sees them seeing her and keeps her eyes down. She walks holding her mother's hand, but neither tugs it to change their trajectory, nor pulls it to bring her mother to a stop. To do so would cause her mother to notice the girls on the sidewalk, and then she might say: "Look, Veronica! Aren't those girls in your class? Say hi, Veronica. Hi, girls! Look, it's Veronica! Yoo hoo!"

So Veronica allows their trajectory to proceed uninterrupted, even though it dooms her.

When it happens, it's like this:

FIRST GIRL
(all one word)
HiVeronica.

VERONICA
Hi.

SECOND GIRL
Hi, Veronica.

Hi.

First Girl says it fast, mean. Hard to detect if you don't know what you're listening for. Veronica answers flat both times. Second Girl says it "neutrally," as in Switzerland.

Whip pan to medium close-up for the jump-cut: Cartoonish Swiss Banker Type, large-ish, square-ish head and shoulders, dark hair, dark moustache, round wire-rim specs, Carl Jung-ish, Swiss cross above the word *Bank* in hanky lettering on sign over shoulder. Close-up on open safe deposit box and sound of rattling as SBT shakes molar-shaped gold nuggets like a Klondike panner. Voice-over: "*Jewish* teeth? Who knew?" Whip pan back to Jess's face, extreme close-up, teeth bared in slight grimace, for a nice match cut.

Then this happens all at once: Veronica and her mother turn the corner, the two girls pass Jess and her baby carriage, and Jess pivots the carriage on its rear wheels so that she is now pointed in the opposite direction, following them, and moving pretty fast.

The wheels of the carriage, of course, appear to be spinning triple-time, backward.

Ahead of her, the girls' spines are military straight. Their vagal nerves have detected a pursuer, but their higher brains are still only registering *mommy with baby carriage*, and so they do not flee. Then their steps speed up, knees locking like speedwalkers', especially when they hear Jess's footfalls, but because their ears also register the rubbery murmur of the carriage wheels, they still don't break into a run.

So Jess catches up with them without changing her stride, and is right behind them when she whispers: "I saw that you nasty girls. I heard that you mean, nasty girls. I don't think that's cool. I don't think it's cool to hate someone. Who taught you it's cool to hate someone, you nasty little girls? I don't think it's cool or grown-up or teenager-ish. It's dogpoop-ish, is what it is," she is trying to say everything she can without actually swearing, "and how would you like it if—"

And here Jess cuts off because the two little girls suddenly bolt into an easement overgrown with *Spiraea nipponica*. The dirt path of the leafy tunnel is knobbly with tree roots and rocks the size of babies' heads.

It's not the Odessa steps, but Jess thrusts the baby carriage after them, straight down the bumps of the easement.

The screaming doesn't come from the little girls, who are well ahead of the carriage. (Their exit from the easement leaves behind a leaf-framed, horizontally trisected square: top, blue sky; middle, asphalt; bottom third, cement sidewalk.) It comes from out of frame. It's not so much loud and long, as repetitive: *Aaah! Aaah! Aaah!*

Jess high-steps it over the roots and babyheads of the easement pathway. Ahead of her, the spinning of the carriage wheels slows as they bump gently over roots, rocking the carriage arhythmically from side to side. Jess reaches out and grabs the handle of the carriage before it too goes out of frame, before it really is the Odessa steps. Catching up to it, she pops a mild wheelie then she and the carriage emerge from the *Spiraea* tunnel.

The yelling is still coming in regular bursts from a woman standing on the front step of a house adjacent to the easement. She is holding the two little girls close to her own body, one hand flat on each of their flat chests. *Aaah! Aaah!*

She's a fear screamer. Some people shut up when they're afraid, some swear and curse. This one's a yeller—not the kind that's best cast in a chainsaw horror, more the inarticulate, backwards-crawling arachnophobe being swarmed by giant tarantulas type.

When the yeller sees Jess, she breaks away and rushes her, asking, "Is the baby all right? Is the baby all right?" She and Jess reach into the carriage at the same time, the woman getting her hands in around the sides of the swaddled blankets before Jess can intercept.

When she hoists it up, the thermos comes away from the bonneted cantaloupe.

Extreme close-up on the woman's face reacting to the headless body she holds before her. Cut away to the cantaloupe head in the carriage, safe on the pillow. Jump cut: the thermos, the cantaloupe, the woman; thermos cantaloupe woman. Zoom out as it registers that the baby she holds at arm's length, a bit above shoulder height, is not only uninjured, but is also a thermos; the brain getting fooled as though it wants to be, even if it has to lie to itself to do it.

Now in medium close-up:

WOMAN
What. The fuck. Is this?
(arms elbow-locked, holding thermos baby out like it's a pooper)

And cut.

She could have gone with her first idea: the thermos spinning slow-mo, end-over-end in an arc against the sky above the woman's outstretched arms, the unexploded grenade with the pin already pulled, a voice-over *Noooooooo* following it, slowed down to Godzilla pitch.

Naw. Clichéd. So Jess says, "I'm a … I'm practising having a baby."

"You're having a baby," the woman repeats.

"I'm practising," says Jess.

"Practising."

The absence of soundtrack music is good here: just bird sounds and cicadas stridulating.

The thermos dangles from the finger the mommy has hooked through the loop handle of the plastic cup. The little girls come running toward her. "Mommy!" It's the first little girl, the one who hates Veronica. "Mommy, that lady—"

"Be quiet, Emily," says the mommy. "Not now."

"But Mom, that lady chased us. She swore at us—"

"I most certainly did not," puts in Jess. She still hasn't moved from her place near the carriage.

"Emily, what are you talking about?" The woman just barely has her ear turned toward her daughter, keeping her eye on Jess instead. Jess shifts focus from the mom's face, close-up, foreground, to the girl's face and back. The shifting blur is nice.

"That lady with the carriage chased us and—"

Emily's mother turns fully toward Jess, her head tilted way to one side, her eyes narrowed.

Jess lets the silence last one beat only, then says: "Emily told her friend—what's your name?" Jess turns to the other girl, to Second Girl, to get the details straight.

"Emma."

"Right." Jess turns back to Emily's mom, "Emily says to Emma that she hates Veronica, and then both of them said hi to Veronica anyway! And Veronica was with her mom!"

Jess realizes there is not a grown-up in sight: not her, certainly not the two girls, and even the woman holding the thermos baby, even she is looking lost. In their little triangle, they are a constellation of bewilderment.

The one working the hardest, at least judging by the effort shown on her face, is Emily's mother, the woman with the thermos.

"Emily," she says, keeping her eyes on Jess, "who is Veronica?"

No answer.

"Emily."

"She's in our class." It's Emma who says this.

"Why would you say you hate her, Emily? And then say hi to her?"

"Mommy," Emily's whisper is horrified, "you do it all the time." The look on Emily's face is the one that comes the first time or two a kid finds out about the double standard. Excellent POV shot.

Jess keeps her gaze on First Girl's face, on Emily's face, a long time, long past comfortable. She breaks the discomfort by stepping into the frame, kneeling into it, really, down toward Emily.

"Would you like to hold the baby?" She's asking Emily, but holding her arms toward the mommy. Jess accepts the thermos baby from the mom, handed to her wordlessly, and passes it to Emily.

Emily takes the thermos baby and, without any trace of sarcasm, tucks it into the crook of her arm.

"Come on, Emma," Emily says. "Let's have a tea party with the baby." The two of them, First Girl and Second Girl—now three, counting the baby—dash around the corner of the house.

A nice long tracking shot to follow the girls, then the pullback picks up the women again; the movement of the camera's gaze through space mimics the passage of time, growing up.

Emily's mommy and Jess are left with the baby carriage and each other. Things are as weird as before. When a car driven slowly past them by a hunched senior slows down, it is only so that the driver can beam an approving smile out to the two women and the carriage. Deep focus here, so both planes are clear and sharp, slow enough to register both car and driver, Jess and mommy. Add a small dog pissing, with muscular back legs outstretched, tiny pelvis lowered so the puddle spreads onto the dog's own toes. The leash extends from behind a bush, attached to an invisible master, screened from view. The invisible master barks, "Come, Sergei!" and Sergei barks in response, kick-kicking hind paws, just for the MacGuffin of it, spreading his scent pointlessly on the concrete, poor beast.

"It must take a lot of practise," offers Jess.

"Yes, yes it does," agrees Emily's mommy.

"Would you like to, uh … ?" Jess gestures toward the carriage.

"Oh!" says Emily's mommy.

Jess reaches into the carriage and hands her the cantaloupe.

"Thank you," she says, accepting it uncertainly.

"Go on," says Jess.

"What?"

"Go on, give it a kiss."

Emily's mommy does not, but then she sees Jess laughing. Not unkindly. She laughs back, unable to resist.

"Awwww, who's the cutest little melonhead?" schticks Jess, making a pout at the cantaloupe in the other woman's hand.

"Who's my little orange watermelon?"

"Cootchie cootchie coo," coos Emily's mom, catching on.

"Nice baby! Nice baby!" says Jess. "Nap time."

Emily's mom gets it and puts the cantaloupe back into the carriage.

"Practise, huh?" she says.

"Yeah," says Jess. "Like what to do if I'm walking along behind two little girls, one of whom decides that a good way to bond with her friend would be to target another little girl as a hate object and then persecute her. Ha, ha! Ha, ha!" She says the whole thing cheerfully, and her laugh is such that Emily's mom laughs back at her, still unable to resist, but not entirely sure why. It must be Jess's delivery.

"I was wondering if you were a crazy bag lady," Emily's mom says.

"Nope. No bag," says Jess.

The other woman says nothing, but her eyes slide toward the carriage and the sleeping cantaloupe.

"Look," says Jess, feeling some urgency. "Don't you ever just get an idea for something and then just go out and do it?"

"No."

It occurs to Jess that this might be the whole problem. So she says, "I must admit my biggest fault is laughing at my own jokes."

"Is that what this is? A joke?"

The mommy looks around, twisting at the waist, and Jess realizes she is looking for television cameras.

"Oh! No, it's just me," says Jess. "No cameras."

"Have you done stuff like this before?"

"Pushed a baby carriage after some little kids? Not that one in particular, no."

"Uh … what have you done?" The woman's eyes are narrowed to slits again.

"Oh!" cries Jess. "The baby!"

She makes a mad dash for the backyard where the girls are playing.

Emily's mom is quick behind her, and she cuts in front of Jess and through the open gate.

In the sandbox, the girls Emily and Emma have made a sand bassinet for the thermos baby and are patting a sand blanket over it. They don't speak and have the serious, almost grumpy faces of children in deep play.

The mommy stops short.

"They're beautiful," whispers Jess to the mommy.

Both women watch silently.

"I should get you your thermos back," Emily's mother says after a while.

The thought of twisting off the plastic cup and hearing the sound of grit in the threads sets Jess's teeth on edge. "No, that's okay," she says. "You keep it. Let the girls keep it."

Jess leaves the mommy standing at the edge of the sandbox, but when she turns to take a last look at the gate, the woman is crouching down to tuck the thermos baby more firmly into bed.

It's more trouble than it's worth to force the carriage back up into the easement, so Jess sticks to the sidewalk, strolling along a little aimlessly until she can find her new direction.

Her gaze broadens, panning wide.

The park is in front of her, an open expanse, and Jess's heart and body leap a little at the sight of it. She brings the carriage to a stop and stands there, breathing in the green air. Soft, so soft, the ambient light made green by the trees, and the sweetness of sound. Anything can happen, she feels. Maybe she will decide to get pregnant, or maybe she'll go on practising. Maybe she'll make a movie.

She's looking for Veronica, of course, or for Veronica and her mom. When she sees them, she starts the carriage wheels rolling.

Revelation

She feels the sharp points at her temple—metal? Glass?—and rolls her face into the floor to get away from them, but this is worse: the sharp points pierce her brow. So, in spite of the bulk of her pregnancy, she heaves herself to sitting. She sees stars.

They are not the gold floating specks that have been in her vision since her second trimester; these stars are tiny clusters of ground glass. They are on a wire circlet which is wound inexplicably around her forehead. She can just see it if she rolls her eyes upward far enough to get a headache.

Her hands go to the crown of stars. She runs her fingertips around the circlet, moving her hands together because they are bound. She starts at the back of her head, moves above her ear, across her forehead, above the other ear. There the skull has swollen up in a ridge like tectonic plates at a fault line. She closes her eyes, keeps her fingertips to the stars, circumnavigates her skull, and counts the clusters: twelve.

She does not think *what?* She does not think *the?* She does not think any words at all. Maybe the mind shuts itself down in parts, louvering the doors as a way to manage reality.

The doors open a little, and now this is what she knows: She had been holding office hours. Nothing unusual. That kid, Bobby, had shown up. Finally. Complaining about a bad mark for a bad paper.

Here in the dark, his face is suddenly there. A brief flash. And with it, something else comes true—she is still at the university. It smells of clean concrete.

She could be in a stairwell or in one of the cavernous rooms below ground level, the mock soundstages where film and television students set up equipment and shoot their assignments. It's not completely dark: light leaks in from under a door. Her eyes adjust.

All right. She is still at the university. The student, Bobby, had been in her office.

She had been surprised when his name showed up on her class list. It's a name that gets passed around the faculty lounge. He's talented and smart, but is dismissed as generally crazy. He's a nightmare to have in tutorial, using every assignment to condemn the university.

Her field is culture and technology—these days, reality TV and the search for fame even at the price of public humiliation. And Facebook: technology nailed to a cross of narcissism. But she also teaches a first-year course on the Bible, for students who need the background for literature, art, film. She teaches the Old Testament as mythology, the New Testament as a history of the Bible, calling it *Loading the Canon.*

She tells her students this little humanist university, with the faculty floating on it, is a tiny island of secularism in a growing sea of fundamentalism. On this little island, we drift with a growing awareness that our assumptions are turning out to be wrong, that secularism is not spreading with development and democracy. All those conservative politicians waiting for the Rapture, working it into their foreign policy.

Bobby doesn't laugh, even though she has made the joke knowing he might be the only one in the lecture hall to get it.

So what is he doing in her course? It's like he's planted himself there, like some kind of terrorist. He knows the Bible as well as she does.

She can hear humming, ticking, something like dripping. The building is alive with electricity, plumbing, the mumbled roar of its life support. Her wrists are bound in front of her, but she can push herself along. Shuffling carefully on her bottom, she finds a wall to lean against, hangs her head. She lets images enter, keeps them wordless.

The baby she carries—a boy, she knows from the ultrasound—turns heavily inside her. When she saw him on the technician's dark screen, his spine looked as beautiful as a constellation, a string of luminous pearls hurled against a night sky.

The kid named Bobby. Not a kid, not with that much facial hair. He is very angry. She watches this memory in the dark like it's a silent movie. In her small office, he stands while she sits. She is too heavy to stand quickly or comfortably, and she no longer cares to play status positions. She is in charge. The kid knows this. He can't get her to change the mark.

And now something like a soundtrack accompanies the reeling pictures. Bits of conversations, lectures, presentations, papers:

the image becomes not real but reality / exists in the imagination / is real to the imagination / creates belief / science / religion / foreign policy / the Bible / mythology mistaken for history / failure of secularism / necessity of poetry / the image in words / made to mean anything by those who control meaning / no objective observer / no facts / hunger poverty war / tell those who suffer / mistake poetry for history / the image becomes not real but reality / belief is created / don't you believe in / don't you believe

If belief creates meaning, why is your poetry more real than anyone else's? It sounds like something she would say in a lecture. In fact, it was the question he'd asked her. A kid like Bobby would say humanism is just another mythology mistaken for history. But then, he's crazy. Not because of his Christianity, but certainly not in spite of it, either. Just along side it.

In her office, Bobby shouts, "Don't you believe in God?" with his essay rolled like scripture, raised like a club, and she laughs. He knows she doesn't. She ponied up to it at the beginning of the course. He has revealed himself to be the biased, irrational, righteous bully she suspects them all of being. Freeze frame: her head back in an exasperated, rude, triumphant guffaw.

Only not triumphant. Inside the rolled essay is something heavy enough to slam consciousness from her when it connects with her face.

And now she is here in semi-darkness, without words. Hands bound, barefoot. She has been adorned with hideous finery and she is carrying an eight-month pregnancy.

This is when she hears the sound of metal on concrete. "Get up."

She is very still, her hands in front of her face like a portcullis. He grabs her by the arms, pulls her to standing. Something very hard is rammed into the small of her back, the part of her spine that flattened out its curvature as the baby took up room inside her. Bobby shoves her ahead of him through the doorway. The gun slides across her hip to where she imagines the baby's head to be, and Bobby reaches in front to free her wrists. Nylon webbing, a plastic lock, released with a plastic key.

The new room is full of light from the 500-watt tungsten bulbs used for shooting Super 8 or sixteen millimetre. The lights are pointed at a set. Hanging from the grid is a heavy canvas drop cloth, painted blue-black and star studded. A plaster crescent moon the size of a cradle sits on the floor, on the cloth.

He nudges her toward the moon, gets her standing behind it.

When he starts to mess with the shoulders of her dress, she gets it. The lights are unbelievably hot. She is to be clothed with the sun. And this is how he's going to do it.

With all the grace she can bring, she steps backward onto the drop cloth, even taking his arm for a moment for balance. Then she shrugs out of the button-front dress and front-close bra. She pauses, struggling slightly with her underwear, her spine without any place to flex this far into the pregnancy. She pulls the underwear down, one side then the other, past her thighs, and when the waistband gets close to her knees she pushes them with her fingertips until they drop, and she toes them aside.

She stumbles but then is sure as she steps up onto the plaster moon and he comes around to the front to face her. The moon is heavy: it does not rock as she plants her bare feet firmly, slightly apart. She stands there, the heat of the lights on her naked skin, her face toward their brightness and her eyes closed.

She is in awe of it, this thing he has made.

She knows what comes next in Revelation 12:1, and she knows he does too.

"And there appeared a great wonder in heaven …"

It's a recorded voice. He must have turned it on.

"… a woman clothed with the sun, and the moon under her feet, and upon her head a crown of twelve stars. "

She's in awe of how much he has had to do to make this happen. That's all. She's not in awe because she's been saved.

With her palms cupping the brightness from the lights, she tips her head to the side, lets her eyes close again, breaks her silence:

"How's this?" she asks.

"What?"

"I get it, I get it. Clothed with the sun ... crowned with stars ... the moon. I am the woman. The great wonder—" Make him think she's playing along with it. "Shall I turn this way?" Turning. "If the lights weren't so bright, I could see better ... What are you going to do now?"

"I'm going to film you."

"I know that. But how long do I stand here after you get the shot? Am I supposed to stand here until I go into labour?"

"I'm not talking to you."

"You are, actually. I'm a person. I'm here."

"I'm supposed to film you and then kill you."

She lets this sink in, not breathing as it does.

"Kill me."

A nod.

"Like some kind of biblical snuff film."

Nod.

"That's stupid."

But then the kid—the boy, the man—is on his knees, crying. His face is pressed into the floor, and he rolls his forehead on the starry drop cloth. He crawls around on the floor, moaning and sobbing and crawling. It's hard for her to make out the words. Still with her palms cupping the brightness from the lights, she tips her head to the side, lets her eyes close again, turns her ear and listens.

"I'm supposed to film you," he moans. "I'm supposed to film you giving birth and kill you."

At first, because of the crying, she hears *fimmoo* and *kiyoo*. Sobs. Then, "You're going to do a birth video?" This ignites a feeling

136

like a small sun inside her chest. Her eyes open. At her feet, Bobby's fingers are spread on either side of his bowed head. On the floor beside one hand, a child's plastic recorder lies white on the painted night sky, the word *Angel* printed in gold below the mouthpiece, in the same gold as the stars. Angel Recorders.

This little shit has kidnapped her with the end of a toy.

She takes one step back and down, crouches grotesquely to heft the plaster moon up and away from her belly. "Bad!" she cries, hoisting the moon high in her outstretched arms. "Boy!" she shouts as the moon comes down. "Don't." Smash. "You." Smash. "Fuck." Smash. "With me." Smash, smash.

The first blow of the plaster crescent moon makes him buckle, and he is still after that. The balance of smashing and shouting occurs as she skates in the greasy blood on the drop-cloth sky. She slips, stumbles, falls.

She is on her hands and knees in her sweat and his blood, the broken plaster moon soaking up the red to make pink chalk. She pants, and she's crying, too. She's safe then. She's safe. The baby is safe.

Then, what? She grips a piece of broken plaster and arches. A contraction?

The doors to the soundstage clunk open, the safety bars clanging like heavy bells. The magnet stops that hold the doors are level with her eyes. She watches the doors move toward the srops, stay. Feet enter, equipment is rolled in. She can't speak because of another contraction, but almost passes out from relief. She's saved.

In relief, she rolls on her side. She no longer feels the twelve starry clusters pressing into her temples and forehead, she is that numb. The contractions don't come again. Just shock, then: She's been kidnapped. She's killed a person. All these things in words, the words making distance. Shock making her legs shake. She plucks at her fallen dress, pulls it across herself.

She closes her eyes. She listens to the people who have come to save her move about the room. Lets the floor hold her up. Waits for an IV needle to enter her arm or a blood-pressure cuff to be wrapped or a stethoscope to be pressed to her chest or hands to raise her.

Finally, she opens her eyes. The dark shoes that have come in the door stand beside hinged metal cases on casters. Two pairs. Three. The metal cases are shut tight, the shoes are not white, and no one moves. No one moves to help her. The shoes step over Bobby. Toward her.

Now, hands do reach for her. Gently, but not to help. A man on either side, they move her into position so she rests on her elbows and knees. Is that a contraction? It can't be. Not now.

The shoes step away.

What she hears next is, "Roll camera." And the lights get brighter.

Behind her, a hieratic voice, intoning something. She doesn't care what. She is going into labour, and the first hard contractions are so hard she is without breath or voice.

Then screams which she thinks, at first, are hers. The lights get even brighter.

But the screams are coming from the men. They are stumbling, crying out in their deep voices. She raises her head. They don't look at her. They are backing away from the body of Bobby, or rather, they are backing away from where his body was. It's gone.

"Praise Him! Praise Him!" one of the bodies connected to the shoes shrieks, voice gone high as a mother's. "Hallelujah! It's the Rapture."

The voice is going up and up, in pitch and literally too. She can see the hard soles of their dark shoes as they rise toward the ceiling.

Then they too are gone—the good, bad men—and she is left behind. With her baby, with her body, with the good, good earth.

Flight

This is it, thought Barton in flight.

The boy he had followed into the washroom had on those pants that were either way too big for him or meant to look too big. Baggy, irritating, disrespectful. Barton had followed him, but only because he had to use the can himself. There was the kid—how old? Six? Nine? Ten? Great big undone basketball shoes, sloppy sloppy sloppy. And he was standing there in front of the sink, not in front of the urinal, but in front of the sink, as if he had come in just to wash his hands or something sissy like that.

Barton's glance swept the stalls, the spaces between doors and floor. No one there.

In one arc Barton pulled his turtleneck up over his nose and his ball cap lower over his eyes. On the follow-through, his forearm vectored to enclose the boy's insubstantial chest, levering the kid's back against his, Barton's, gut. The kid's breath left with a noise that Barton stifled with his palm, pinching the kid's nostrils with thumb and forefinger. His other hand, the one that reached across the kid's chest, cupped the fine round ball of the boy's shoulder and caressed it. Barton's long fingers brushed down.

The kid didn't struggle. Some didn't. Barton was good at picking the ones who wouldn't. It was like a talent. A gift. A natural ability to really know things about a person, to understand that person in just a glance. He was rarely wrong. His friends knew this about him, and it made them a little afraid of him, in a good way. He wanted people to know that he wasn't someone to be fooled with, that his job was just a job and maybe even a front; his double agency being something he hinted at, but was careful never to reveal. This was a good way to keep people off balance. People *should* be afraid of him—even if they didn't know why, they should. His co-workers were *right* to be wary, right to get up and leave when Barton sat down at the lunch table at break time. It made him smile into his sandwich—hiding it in the bite. Their butts lifting off the bench like it was red hot when he sat down, as if the specialness of his arse made the aluminum glow. The idea of this always made him want to laugh out loud, but he didn't, the guffaw puffing out around the food in his mouth instead. He ate with gusto, "loving his meats," as his nan had said. It was an appearance, in fact, for Barton had no sense of taste or smell.

Which was maybe why he was able to even go *into* some of the toilets this city saw fit to pass whatever lame-ass health inspections they were subject to. But Barton had seen the half-wits, the immigrant broom-pushers, and the zitty teenagers whose job it was to clean them, so he guessed it was all that could be expected.

The boy's buttocks were surprisingly small inside the underwear once Barton's wrist slipped in past the elastic waistband. There was so much manoeuvring room inside the seat of the pants, in fact, that Barton was able to get his message across before withdrawing because of a flushing sound from one of the stalls.

Fuck. He'd checked it. It was so natural to him that he didn't even second-guess: he knew he'd checked it and that no feet had shown below the doors. He checked again, anyway. Christ. Busted toilet. The stupid thing flushed on its own again while he peered under the stall door. Typical of a place like this, typical of the substandard state of the physical plant. No safe place for a kid to use the can anywhere in this city, without having a broken toilet explode up into his privates while he's doing his business.

But the moment was ruined anyway. Barton was irked, and whatever satisfaction he might have been able to expect from showing some kid that you always had to be on your guard, always, was ruined by the noise of the faulty toilet that destroyed the atmosphere of trust and communication he had been trying to establish in the quickest way possible.

"Pull up your pants, kid. Tie your shoes. Straighten your hat. You're a mess, for Christ's sake." He'd gotten that much across, at least, before slipping out into the concession area, a little echoey now because intermission was over and the stands were full again with loud fans, dads and boys on a Saturday morning.

Barton figured, both from calculations and from close calls in the past, that he had roughly five minutes to get done what he needed to get done before someone would be able to decipher what some messy-faced kid was trying to blabber out. Then several more minutes, depending on whether the kid was a lardass or well dressed or gussied up like a movie star's kid or a number of other variables. Barton knew that good-looking kids got attention faster, and so the very best ones were fat and had glasses; with luck they had some kind of spitty lisp or couldn't say R or W properly.

He had learned from when he'd stuck around to help look, or simply hung back in the crowd a bit, that the really pathetic ones were not believed at all, even if they pointed right at him and bawled.

This time, because the kid was still motionless in the washroom where he had left him, Barton figured he had close to double the normal time to complete his transformation and get on his way.

The kid would have to come out, find the grown-up in the stands who'd brought him, convince the dad or uncle or brother or what have you, then try to get the grown-up to move move move if, that is, there was going to be a pursuit. Which, the vast majority of the time, there wasn't.

It was the ease of the job that attracted him. After the first few times, he'd honed his plan and correctly calculated times and clothing choices, sometimes using a stopwatch to work up his speed.

But.

Wait.

Here was a man, hands in pockets, looking up at the I-beam rafters arching above the entranceway to the stands. He had his mouth pursed a bit, but wasn't exactly whistling, and he was moving in a slow circle as he gazed up.

Barton knows instantly, in the way he does, from his place of jungle instinct—like he can practically read minds for fuck's sake, like he has more than X-ray vision to see right in your head and read your mind, like he's everywhere, behind you, ahead of you, beside you, even in the sky over your head or, this time, above the metal girders that support the roof, darting among the I-beams and their rivets furred with hot-dog fumes and dirt so thick that he could write his name in it, dragging his fingernail in the guck and striking oil—Barton knows instantly that the man is the kid's father.

Fancy leather ball cap, like the boy's, leather jacket, leather boots. Hair trim trim trim around the close beard as though the guy were at the barber every other day. Barton could practically see through the pocket of the soft brown jacket, into the fist of fingers curled carelessly around the keys to a beamer or an Audi or a godforsaken Hummer or just a dumb-fuck van renamed SU fucking V, bigger than a mobile home—like the guy needs a fucking all-wheel drive to get up the Bridle Path to his six-figure mansion full of multimedia this and that for the spoiled kid who doesn't even have the decency or manners to pull up his goddamn pants in public, like his parents are too fucking fancy and out of it—parties, drugs, swimming pools, wife-swapping, group frigging orgies—to teach the kid some respect.

The man, though, is not looking at him. He's looking up. Barton's got his reversible jacket turned inside-out and almost on again, and the man is just starting to move his head, like he's heard Barton's soft-soled shoes—impossible—or maybe sensed motion or caught something in his peripheral vision.

Barton straight-arms through the second sleeve like his fist is a cannonball. He snaps his hand open, releasing the wadded-up ball cap into the wide mouth of the garbage can, hooks a pair of wire-rimmed glasses over one ear then the other with a nod, and is almost at the double doors to the parking lot.

He is not on the ceiling or in the rafters anymore, but can still see around himself in every direction without having to turn his head, but does so anyway, barely, and is vaguely surprised to find that the man is still not looking at him, but is, in fact, staring at the handle of the men's room door.

Even so, Barton is calm, knowing he can count on bawling time. His step is quick but short. The guy maybe saw him leave the men's room, maybe not. He'll be through the parking lot before the guy can even get a story out of the kid. There's no need to run.

The feeling he gets now, of leaving the ground and stepping lightly with a slight bounce on an invisible trampoline a foot or so above the ground, is one well known to him. A long time ago, when it first started, he had been stupid enough to tell the doctor about it. He has since come to know that this feeling is called elation, and that he gets it when he knows it's a job well done: that kid in the washroom, he'll think twice about going out in public dressed like a bum or a hoodlum. What's this crazy shit about pretending to be poor or tough when you're neither, no matter how much money your old man loses on the stock market or wherever he robs people blind and gets paid for it?

Barton is through the heavy double doors. The air of the blue day is cool in his strong lungs. He breathes deeply, filling his chest, feeling the feeling of rising. The kid might even thank him, someday. Ought to thank him. He'll look back at this as a turning point in his life. It's a matter of pride. You have to walk like you deserve respect if you're going to get it, and that means dressing right and having some manners. And maybe he'd shown the kid that. In his own small way, he'd shown the kid that you get what you deserve. Hell, the kid hadn't cried. Barton recollected the look on the kid's face when his middle finger had gotten the kid's attention, and, upon reflection, besides a little startled, the kid had only looked grateful.

Barton hears gravel beneath his shoe soles, but knows his sensation of hovering above the parking lot is truer than what is visible to the outside world. The gap between the fence posts opens far away, but near: he will reach it in time. He moves toward it.

Now Barton had been right about some things: The man looking up at the ceiling had neither heard nor noticed Barton leave the men's room, nor had he seen him switch his clothing. The man looking up at the ceiling had only noticed from the corner

146

of his eye that someone—a man, sure, but it could have been anyone—was leaving the building. He had, indeed, been staring in the opposite direction of Barton's trajectory.

But Barton had not the prescience to predict, from the fixed nature of the man's stare, the swiftness with which the man would cross to the door of the washroom, nor the grace with which the man would kneel to encircle the white-faced boy with his arms, nor the speed with which the man would rise with the boy still in his arms and turn, almost in one motion, to move with the boy as though air-lifting him across the concession area, through the double doors and into the parking lot.

There was no way for Barton to know that the man would be saying to the boy the whole time, quietly, evenly, non-stop, from the moment he knelt, through the whole flight path we are following here, "You are a good boy, you are a good boy. You have done nothing wrong. I believe you. And you are safe." Saying it without knowing why yet.

The boy, in fact, stayed silent. His body was taut as a foil.

Barton had been right that the man was the boy's father, though. He was also right that the man housed his family on or near a road like the Bridle Path, that his home had come with a price tag of six very high figures, and that he handled the wealth and privilege of the wealthy and privileged.

To this man, and to the woman he loved, the boy in the baggy pants had been born early and more than a little anxiously: there had been six miscarriages in as many years. After the first two, the woman just stopped talking about it. She stopped talking about it as she smiled and went to her job and worked and came home. They cooked holiday dinners for their families, which expanded

147

exponentially as children were conceived and carried and delivered, seemingly without effort, by sisters and sisters-in-law and cousins and cousins' wives.

The boy's premature birth was a factor, but he likely would have turned out small for his age anyway: light-boned like his mother and on the short side like his father. The father and the mother had been counselled to expect delayed or below normal development, but the boy seemed to grow on schedule, his small stature making him appear to be a precociously early walker, talker, and potty-user. Which he had been, in truth, but his persistent milk cheeks and baby-round body, in conjunction with his precocity, gave him the appearance of a pretty, baby-sized man. His mouth had an oddly adult cast, although from infancy he had smiled and laughed readily, possibly delighted by the absurdity of being alive at all.

More than eight years later, they had conceived again, without thought or intention—they had been given no reason to hope. But there was a baby girl, nonetheless. On this day and at this time, the baby was asleep with the mother, held in arms. Her birth had been markedly different. The man had cut the cord himself, momentarily suspended in a vision of newborn infants who wafted past as though on a current, their umbilical cords trailing beneath their bellies as they scudded along: helium balloons just out of reach of keening men and women who were rooted below, their arms and hands poking through clouds, stretched toward the babies above. The man thought he saw himself and his wife among them. Above her surgical mask the ob-gyn, a friend from university, called him back with a look. He squeezed the sideward-curved scissors, thinking *marshmallow* as they met the resistance of the cord.

With his son in the seat of the pickup truck (Barton had been wrong about the vehicle, a domestic, workable half ton), the man was mostly thinking about getting through the parking lot and out the gate to the express lanes. He did not drive quickly, but gingerly, with the feeling that his son was still deciding whether to stay in his father's grip or to return to the place he had been before he was born; the man was aware that a sudden jolt in a pothole might cause either of them to accidentally let go. So the man held his son's left hand tightly in his right. He knew something had happened. Maybe something terrible, but he didn't know what.

The boy still had not spoken, but would. The father knew this and knew that when he did, the boy would be told, "I believe you."

"I believe you," he would tell the boy, right away. For this is what the man had been gifted with: a form of love that let him trust the child in a way that was not visible to either of them, but was something that felt almost tangible, something that could be gripped. He knew that to some people the difference between feeling-truth and truth-truth was nothing. He could listen to both, and he could hold both, simultaneously, balancing them like spun-glass eggs in spun-glass nests, carrying spun-glass birds with spun-glass hearts that miraculously beat in real time, pumping real life and longing for real flight.

When he would say to his son, "It's going to be all right," his son would believe him, and so then something about it all would be all right. And the boy would believe him, in this way, through the news coverage of his arrest, through the short and awful trial, the publicity, the conviction, the job loss, the jail time, the packing up and selling of the house and its contents, the move to a smaller, greener city, the transfer from private to public schools, and the newness of everything: friends, surroundings, trees, air.

Through the time of the baby taking her first steps, and the mother and the son and the daughter walking in the woods with the dogs, through springtime and summer and autumn and another cycle of these, waiting for the father to rejoin them, waiting and waiting until the father came home, changed, but not as much as you might think. After his return, the man and the woman sometimes would hold hands all through the night in the dark until day came, taking turns sleeping, taking turns being awake.

In the truck, the man was looking at his son. In his peripheral vision he could see the gap in the fence that led from the parking lot to the on-ramp, and he aimed the truck toward it. But his face was turned toward his son's, so he saw his son's eyes lock onto something outside the truck and saw something happen to the flesh of his son's face to make it appear as though the boy were dead. His taut body went slack.

Maybe this is why the man pressed his foot to the gas. Maybe this is why, when he turned his head away from his son to look where he was driving, he saw Barton already parallel to the horizon, already at windshield height. Framed in the gap between the fence posts, one arm extended along the topside of his body, the other below as though to support his head, Barton was tilted slightly skyward, legs scissoring nothing, in the improbable posture of a swimmer sidestroking in midair.

To all three of them, it seemed he was flying.

How It Is

We got caught in a cold rain. The wet ran off my hat and straight down my collar.

—Goddam it! You got a Lucifer?

Lighting his damp hand-rolled under the sheltering brim. The ponies puff out clouds and stamp their feet. He looks hard at my hand that holds the match, so I explain:

—Shot my own hand once, saving my daddy. Got no web to hold my thumb on now.

The smoke is between his lips. Deep draw.

—Your old man a hangman?

Says it clenching the hand-rolled in his teeth.

—Nope. Preacher.

He smokes, so I go on:

—Made us build a church in every town we stopped in. I'd fashion spires from the spokes of busted wagon wheels. Poke 'em up into the sky to snag God on as he went flying by haw, haw.

—God don't fly.

—The hell he don't.

We ride.

—What if you could fly? What if you could hold on to God's tail and fly through the air? Would you do it?

We are heading northeast. For some time we have been aiming for the green fringe on the horizon that marks the edge of the valley we are about to fall into. He don't know it.

I say:

—You is called Crinkles. What's your right name?

—Not sayin'.

—Well then, why do they call you Crinkles?

He grins and lifts his hat offen his head. Puts it down again over what's underneath.

He cuts his eyes toward me and says:

—My real name is Jesus.

He pronounces it *Hey Zeus*, but I think about it for a moment and say:

—I reckon it is more common south of the border.

We are cutting the Qu'Appelle now, south to north, east of the old Espérance pemmican fort. It's narrow and the river is not much here.

Above the prairie we are crossing on this drizzling night, a little god is flying through the clouds roughly. The coarse hairs on his body snag droplets of water and ice in the grey-black fog so that his passage is mapped by a line of fine spray. The cowboy would not see the little god, even if he looked up.

Not that I see him neither, but I know. And he leaves a trail.

Out of habit, or perhaps as a symptom of his existence, the little god redirects the flight of birds as he passes, and so, temporarily, a flock of wild geese abandon their V-formation and orbit instead in a vertical ellipsoid, turning their white breasts up to heaven.

I turn my horse and so must he, so the little god and his shenanigans is to our backs. We are almost there.

—This part here, these burr oaks, it could be Mamre, and us on our way to Sodom.

Crinkles rides with his head down, hands gripping the saddle horn, and I wonder if he is sleeping.

Now we come up out of the valley, our horses plodding head down too. Up on the prairie, I say to him, because it is not a question:

—We're heading for the spy hill.

He folds in a bit, as though struck softly in the chest with an axe. The locked box is in the blanket roll behind my saddle. If I took a look, I might see it glowing, but I know it ain't, so I don't.

And the little god, what does he do? He begins to scratch, as though infested with fiery fleas. I can feel his itch.

The rain is still coming down, and the sky is low, but we can see the spying hill a least ways off, to the east.

—That it?

The little god is grinning, and each scratch of his long nails causes his hide to ripple. You will know, of course, that the little god is daemon, the genius that resides in each of us, the animus spiritus that wants what it wants whether we will or not. Each of us has one—at least one. The little god does not know what the cowboys will do next. But it knows what it wants.

It is around this time I always ask them what they wish they'd done, and they always tell me.

I do, and he does:

—I never had me a little baby, never had a little son. I wanted a little baby so much. Don't laugh. I ain't womanish. Just always thought a little baby would be 'bout the best present I could get.

—Yeah? What would you do with a baby?

Nothing.

—You know what you'd do with a baby? You'd eat it, that's what.

He looks sorrowful 'cause he knows I am right.

The hill rises up from out of nowhere. It is three hills, really, in a humpy sprawl. I think when we get there I will push the cowboy from his saddle and he will lie like that.

Now, with the hill so near, the rain stops and the worser clouds tear themselves apart and dissolve on the wet sky. There ain't no sunset. We missed it, and it's too early for stars. It's just flat dark.

The little god flies in a seated position, knees bent up and sit-down place scudding along some unseeable plane. His tail curves under, following the line of his haunch, then torques downward. The end hairs pull flat out in the wind. I do not want to look, but I do, checking. Uh huh. He's up there.

When we get down from our horses, I take Crinkles and lay him back just like an empty dress. I take the box from out my bedroll and put it above his head. He makes a sighing noise, the air leaving a concertina squeezebox then rusting back in. I put my boot on his chest, push down, let the air in his lungs raise it up again, push down, playing a song on him. Wheeze, draw, wheeze, draw.

All along the trail from Big Muddy, I believe the man in the next saddle to be the most beautiful friend I have known. There's a daguerreotype of me and each of them. Sometimes we is holding hands. I always have my jacket open so you can see my gun. My great grandniece has those pictures in her parlour. Go see them. You can go and see them. They're in her parlour. Most of what I have done in my life I have done for my own little god. It ain't my fault I am what I am.

Crinkles's back arches up away from the wet grass, boot heels digging. The crown of his ten-gallon hat don't provide much grip-tion, and Crinkles slams back to earth with a thud and a grunt. Then he's at it again, banging on the ground faster and faster, his feet now starting to pelt in an unsteady, annoying rhythm. He's saying *unh, unh, unh,* and his hands are scrabbling in mud and low grass, trying to get purchase.

Just as he's ending, the little god lands. He has been hovering above spy hill for a long while, dangling his tail loosely down. Now, with hind feet narrow and bony on the earth, he stands with knees still bent and pointing outward. I can tell he is discomfited by the stance, him not being accustomed to going on the ground.

I take hold of the rope around Crinkles's neck. It is frayed from where I cut him down.

The little god teeters toward us on the outsides of his clawed feet. He rocks back and forth as he progresses and reaches one long arm and one long-fingered hand out to take the end of the rope. He jerks the rope once or twice, but the prone cowboy only groans. So the god lifts a hind leg over the rope, straddling it. It protrudes from between his thighs. He looks at me.

I come around to the backside of the god, pull the frayed rope end through his legs, and tie it to his tail. He starts to rise up. I see the backside of the god rising up.

That cowboy becomes thinner and paler as he is pulled along behind the god, so that he streams out like a pennant. Soon he is a tatter of cloud.

I watch as they go. Their progress is marked by the movement of the fast cloud, but the little god cannot be seen.

I find that I am holding the box. It is no longer heavy. It is light as light. I open it.

Inside, there is a little baby in pieces. The head, cradled in my palm, is smaller than a plum. I lay the tip of my finger in the wallow between its nose and top lip, think to myself *philtrum.* I don't know why.

The baby's eyes open, stare into mine. Its little mouth opens, three cornered. I bring it to my face. My breath makes the little baby's baby lungs billow out for the first time in eternity—a town lady's skirt raised to the curb, full-up with petticoats; it floats back down to dirt, and the flannels wrap their selfs flat to her legs like bandages.

Into its open mouth, I tell the baby its future. The lips close; the eyes shut. I put the tiny head in my mouth, hold it there a minute with my lips drawn together. I swallow. Then I swallow the other pieces, one by one. The bones are tiny and slide down my throat. Maybe I will be a woman now, I think.

I mount up. The baby in my belly is putting itself together. I can feel it bob with the motion of the horse. Above us, new clouds are gathering. From their darkness, a little hand reaches down, waves its hairy fingers, and retreats.

I have been hanging men for fifteen years, the first one being my own daddy. He crawled up that spire, went up the high tower. Late at night, he went up, found something up there he couldn't live with.

He just never felt so good after that. After a while, I roped him up with the bell rope. I kept up the ringing so I wouldn't hear him choking, and when he wouldn't stop kicking, I used my gun. Killed my own thumb, trying to get my hand to let go the rope. Shot clean through, and down came Daddy.

But with the cowboys, I am gentle. All them rustlers and the killers. First I give 'em what they want most, then I carry all their secrets, keep 'em forever. It ain't their fault they gotta hang, ain't their fault they gotta live those dirty lives. That little god. That dirty little god.

Hockey Jesus, Jesus Hockey

I come from a short line of independent women, dedicated to higher education and the joys of solitary intellectual pursuits. I have an aunt who is a nun, who left home at fifteen with nothing in her suitcase but a pack of cigarettes, a comic book, and her hockey skates to join the convent in Winnipeg, and from her I have fabricated a genealogy of Heloises to non-existent Abelards.

As I get older, I wonder how my life would have turned out had I followed my dreams *then*—at the magical age of fifteen, when I knew my dreams and heart, unlike *now*, when both have been weakened, shot out of a cannon every morning by my aggressively affectionate six-year-old who is pleased to announce that he is awake by kissing my arms and saying, "I am the boy of love. I am made of pure love."

It's supposed to be endearing, and it is, but after several years of it, I suspect that he does it so I won't smack him and holler, "Git the fire goin' in the woodstove," or shriek, "Get it off me!"

These are no longer options, as I have left behind the Saskatchewan farmhouse in which I never really grew up—summer holidays, yes, and some long weekends, but no actual farming with filthy dirt or vegetable plots meant to feed a family of twelve or business of any kind involving frightening, voluminously pooping livestock. There was a woodstove, but I certainly was never allowed to git the fire goin' in it.

As for "Get it off me!" I swore off recreational delirium tremens when I first became pregnant. "Honey!" I cried, taking the last couple hauls off a cigarette. "The test is positive!" *Flush*: the sound of the toilet annihilating my last smoke and the pee stick.

Had I followed my dreams at fifteen, instead of being shamed out of them by my parents—"You want to go to art school? They don't shave! They don't marry!"—I would be closer to being my own nun, which I'm not, than to being a painter, which I'm also not.

Yes, the legacy of brainiac young women leaving the farm for better things, in our family, is strong. I had to piece it together, though, from shouts and side-mouth mutterings squirted from my mother and her sisters when they got together on Saturday nights for that Misery of Miseries to nerds everywhere: *Hockey Night in Canada.*

It was Wednesday nights too, so I was virtually orphaned by the six-team league.

At fifteen, that magical age when a person teeters for seconds at a time on the brink between knowing who she is and having the wherewithal to do something about it, I was stranded in rage, thinking, "Jesus, hockey, hockey, Jesus! Don't these people know there's more to life?"

My mother tells me that her earliest memory is of throwing herself on the bed to weep after listening to *Radio-Canada* and enduring the defeat of les Canadiens at the hands of *les mauvais* Leafs. I am sure it was the bed on which she and her four sisters were born—not all at once, of course—the very bed on which her mother would later succumb to the embarrassingly countrified disease of dropsy.

At fifteen, I compassionately concluded that my grown mother's rabid obsession with hockey, to the neglect of her teenaged daughter, me, was due to one of those death-associations: the bed in which her maman bore her, the bed in which her maman took her last dropsy breath, the bed on which she wept after listening to René Lecavalier say on *Radio-Canada* that the *mauvais* Maple Leafs had beat us. Us!

I assumed dropsy was like that attractiveness-enhancing disease that made Teresa Stratas in *La Traviata* look rosier and rosier cheeked as she sang away, choking for her last breaths, her diaphragm breathing and singing somehow unaffected.

You see, already, at fifteen, I was immersed in Higher Culture, opening a yawning class chasm between me and my less sophisticated parents with their Roger Whitaker albums: What artist chooses to be photographed with their lips pursed? You can't hear the whistle coming out of the album cover. He probably didn't even breathe from his *diaphragum*, which was how I pronounced *diaphragm* along with *chasum* for *chasm*, and *a dole sense* for *adolescence*, the result of having read precociously to myself.

So I tolerated my mother's obsession with hockey until I reached my own a dole sense, when self-centredness bloomed in me like the TB roses in an opera singer's cheeks.

My mom and her four sisters—nuns or widows, all—would crowd onto the four-seater chesterfield, shortness of leg dictating the feet-in-the-air-thing, cigarettes in the lady-grip of fingertips clamped together tightly as thighs, drinks in hand, balanced and unspilled.

That's why there was no clapping: their hands were full. So just kicking and hooting like *Fransaskoise* chimps. When one leaned forward to kick, all five had to lean forward, they were jammed together so tightly.

"C'est le but!" my mother would shriek from her perch, round feet kicking the air. Her slippers having flown the coop during the first power play. *"Hoo hoo! Cournoyer!"*

I would come in and fume silently behind the chesterfield until the noise was over. "Mom, can I talk to you?" Wait, wait. "Mom?" Waitwait. "Mom?"

"Wait till the period is ended."

"Mom, I've been waiting since my period ended." Beat. Like I'm doing stand-up. No laughs. "I've crashed the car, Mom. I'm marrying a Negro, Mom. I'm going to go to art school, Mom. I've given birth to a chicken. Jesus is crying."

I could say anything. Nothing could distract her from The Game. The Jesus crack was because she used to manage our behaviour at Christmas by commenting sorrowfully, "You're making le bébé Jesus cry," if we were bad. She never said much about it during Lent, though, which would really seem to be the time to milk the "Jesus is Crying 'Cuz of You" thing.

Seriously. I was ten before I learned that there was something other than Catholic. Some other culture, some other language, some other religion. I am fluent in Catholic; it is my first language, even before English or French. I thought everyone spoke it. I'd never met a Protestant until we moved to the city, and it went like this:

A Kid: "Hey kid, whereyagoda school?"

Me: "St. Catharine's. Where do you go to school?"

Him: "Holliston."

Huh? He could have been speaking to me in Prairie Dog or Puffin, neither of which I spoke.

Me: "You mean *Saint* Holliston's."

Him: "There's no Saint Holliston you little Catholic faggot. It's a white school. A school for white kids."

Me: "I'm a girl!"

Him: "Lick the bag! Cath-o-lick the bag!"

What the hell?

Equation: Protestant = Crazy.

But reader, I married one. A Protestant.

And he calls me a hobo.

He calls me a hobo because, as a Protestant, he is not adept at spotting us secular, off-duty, nonprofessed nuns.

I am.

In Saskatchewan, one can easily mistake a farm wife for a lesbian or a nun because of the low-maintenance haircuts and good skin—and because of chins that might be just a tiny bit, and in the nicest way possible, a little tiny bit, not furry, exactly, but just sort of indicating that the bearer of that chin is thinking about things other than chin hairs. But secular nuns, like myself, are characterized more by our fondness for living in tiny cell-like bedrooms—as long as they have sinks and high-speed internet—our propensity for solitary intellectual pursuits, and our commitment to higher and higher education, than by our ability to git a fire goin' in anything.

Growing up in Saskatchewan, I was surrounded by good farm wives who were indistinguishable from lesbians and nuns, and no one called *them* hobos.

In Saskatchewan, I am not a hobo. I was born in the age of electric light, and my first computer was a Micom word processor the size of a clothes dryer, but Saskatchewan years are like dog years, so when I "go home" now, I am 329 years old. I left 210 years ago, when I was a mere 119, having never seen an NDPer wear anything but coveralls until I moved to Ontario and learned they come wearing corduroy blazers with leather elbow patches and Rhodes scholarships.

But in Saskatchewan in the 1960s—that is, about three centuries ago—I took baths in a tin tub inside a shack built over the creek so the bathwater drained directly into the fast-moving water about two feet below. It was the old cream house, and it was built over the water so jars of cream could be lowered through cut-out holes in the floor and kept cold by creek immersion until they could be taken to town. Brilliant, eh? Outside the bathtub shack was a potbelly stove on which we heated both bathwater and the water for scalding the hair off pigs after sticking them in the neck as they hung from The Hook.

The NDPers of my youth, formerly CCFers, had no need for elbow-patched corduroy blazers.

But now and here, I am a hobo.

It is my Protestant, Upper Canadian husband's word, as in, "Oh God, I married a hobo"—the time he saw me hunching over the sink, eating baked beans directly out of the can so I wouldn't dirty a dish. And I didn't want them warmed up, so I didn't need to dirty a pot.

I consider myself logical, rational, and, ultimately, frugal, so the choice to eat cold beans from the can, over the sink, seems logical, rational, and home economics-ly sound. But apparently it gets you called *hobo* if you do it hunched over a fancy sink, standing on one of those warm-up kitchen floors. (Next time, I'll put the can down on the flagstone in advance so it can be radiantly heated before I hunch up to the sink for breakfast. Brilliant, eh?)

But the point is, what gets you called a good wife or secular nun in some circles, gets you called hobo in Ontario. Like, in Saskatchewan you go to *The Lake*, in Ontario you go to *The Cottage*; unless you go *Up North*, then the cottage is *The Camp* or *The Cabin*. But southern Saskatchewan is on the same parallel as Thunder Bay, so let's define *Up North*, here.

Listen, I feel bad about something. The use of the *N* word, up there. Up north in this story. Fifteen paragraphs down from the pole. You know: Negro.

Honestly, using that word, at that time, in that household, meant I *wasn't* prejudiced. I was anti-prejudice! It was the 1970s in Saskatchewan, so in the United States, Scarlett was having her corset tightened before the pig roast at Tara, and Melanie was plotting for Ashley. For the time and place—namely, behind the chesterfield during *Hockey Night in Canada* in my mother's house—I was *radical.*

Or so I thought. To really piss them off, I told myself, all I have to do is *like* everything they *hate* and *hate* everything they *like.* I'll be pro-choice, pro-homo, pro anti-sexist-and-anti-racist. I'll hate hockey, and I won't go to church. It'll drive them crazy. I can rebel without ever leaving home.

But I did. Leave home. In a way. I mean, in the way that anybody ever can. Which is can't, really.

I left my mother sitting on the chesterfield in front of the TV with her sisters, waiting for the guy from The Chinaman's to deliver the Saturday night gobble-fest they would bolt down during intermission, the sound of the Danny Gallivan–Dickie Irvin commentary blocking out anything I might have said, whether they were interested in hearing it or not. We look so much alike, my mother and I: when I see my own round feet hovering above the floor as I sit on the sofa, next to my little daughter, whose feet legitimately extend into mid-air, I notice that her feet look just like my mother's and mine—simultaneously roundish, yet pointed at the toe, like trotters—and I feel like I've given birth to myself.

I left the aunts there, too, and I never went to art school, even though I lived around the corner from OCAD for years, and nothing was actually stopping me.

I left the nun there, ready to drive the priest back to the rectory when the game ended, after he had eaten roast beef dinner with parishioners so nervous about Father coming over for supper that they knocked out the gravy boat and had to swear, "*Ste-Marie Joseph St-Jupiter!*" right in front of him. The nuns back to the convent house—full of luxuries like books and bathrooms with locks, even though the bedrooms were no bigger than jail cells—and *Le Bon Père* off to spot-clean his *soutain.*

I left the good wives with their pixie cuts and perfect skin and competence, their ability to do anything—anything—well and fearlessly, from painting a picture to sticking a pig to making wine out of strawberries to caring for a husband paralyzed from the waist down after a tractor accident three years and two babies— only two, thank the *Bon Dieu*—into the marriage and deciding to stay on the farm and run it at a profit, no less.

I am certainly not a Bride of Christ, but I have an insatiable longing to live in a little room and be struck by wonder and miracles and to never, not ever, have to use up brain space thinking about unwanted facial hair and its removal. If I could be my own nun, I would model myself after St. Wilgefortis. Go read *Fifth Business.*

It drives my husband crazy when I hobo-out in the kitchen, when I try to get him to winterize the toolshed so I can live in it, promising him that if he wants to visit me, all he has to do is knock and say, "Little pig, little pig, let me come in ..." I'll let him.

In the toolshed, there will be no TV, no *Hockey Night in Canada*, and no competition from the Canadiens for my mother's love. I hate hockey, but my reasons for it aren't good. You never have to try to go home again, if you never really leave.

The Weather

The day I touched down in Edmonton, I sat on the porch of my sister's house, met her husband, met her baby daughter, and pretended I knew about her life. The neighbour had a mangy little dog named Toto that I ought to have recognized as the beginning of this story.

I said hello and goodbye to my sister's husband, who was on his way to the big-city job that had bought my sister her dream house on an acreage east of Edmonton. My sister's house was brand new brick. It sat on an enormous lawn of fresh sod patches and rose straight up, unshaded. Around it were grids of one-acre plots, waiting for houses to be set down into a subdivision. The ground around them was dirt.

"Central vac! Central vac!" my sister cried in each room as she gave me the tour. I had an image of her and her husband cawing it at each other as a sort of mating call. "Central vac!" she would cry. "Wall to wall!" he'd reply. And after mating, they would coo with their foreheads pressed together, "Minivan, minivan."

I was to sleep in the pink room my sister introduced as the "the girl's room, when she's big enough." There was a boy's room down the hall, blue and baseball-playered, although there was no boy to put in it yet.

So that night I slept in my niece's future bed, a hard, tiny, flat thing, frilly and exactly like the one I grew up with. Like our mother, my sister had provided yards of frills and scratchy lace for her little princess. And so I lay straight and narrow in the confines of filigree and fluff and began the story I had begun each night since I was small to put myself to sleep.

There was a royal feast for the christening of the daughter born to the king and queen, and to the feast came three fairies, who stood over my lacy bed and sprinkled me with dust of gold, of silver, and of something else: another, darker dust. The dust endowed me with gifts that would aid in my eventual escape, and as the first fairy drew yellow dust from a green satin pouch she said, "I endow this child with dreams." And the second fairy sprinkled silver dust from her red velvet pouch on my head and said, "I endow this child with desire." And the third fairy approached my bassinet, took a blue bag from inside her black cloak, reached in with her brittle hand. She held a fistful of dust above me and said, "Dreams and desire are nothing without my gift, so I endow this child with. I endow this child with. I endow this child with."

In my niece's bed, I played it out, hopeful as ever that I would stay awake long enough to learn the ending. As usual, sleep came first. As usual, I was tranced into oblivion by my own story before I could learn what the third gift was. It's like counting sheep.

I awoke in the middle of the night with a familiar childhood beast on my chest. As when I was small, I tested the terror for a moment before opening my eyes to see that there was no cat crouched there, that it was not melting into me, not making itself liquid to enter my chest, not pouring itself through hollow claws, not re-catting itself inside my gut where it would cling like a tumour. Years later I would see a CT scan of the malignant visitor in my father's frontal lobe, crouching where it had slept, curled and waiting, biding its time—and my father's—until it woke and stretched and raked ten years too late for anyone to save his life. The image of that cloudy shape hunched over the pituitary struck me with a dull clang of recognition, a muffled metallic sound that tasted like an iron spoon or the blood from a bloody nose, swallowed. There was something familiar about it that made me feel as though my stomach had dropped suddenly, as though we had hit turbulence.

But in my niece's bed in Edmonton, the cat on my chest leapt off as I opened my eyes. The room was suddenly filled with odd light. A night fire? I got up and opened the curtains. It was quiet: no trucks or sirens. A sunrise too hot for dawn, more like sunset, but in the east, definitely. The light streaked the horizon in an even line, forced down to the earth by the flat black palm of cloud above it.

I watched as the colour disappeared. It did not fade so much as disintegrate, breaking up into patches like soiled dressings from a wound. Rags of black and red cloud dissolved, leaving the pale blue-green pre-dawn. I heard my sister's husband leave for work as I began again, *There was a royal feast for the christening* … Waking dusty headed later that morning, I kept to myself what I had seen, believing in it as much as I believed in fairies or midnight cats.

But in the afternoon the sky began to bleed once more. The black bandage cloud came down again to staunch the flow, to stop it from leaking into heaven, pressing red velvet against the dark horizon line.

It was dark and beautiful in the distance. A little closer, smoky grey clouds rolled in the sky like giant kittens and, freakishly, the sky directly above my sister's house was mystery milky blue, strange and Siamese. When fist-sized hailstones began to thump lazily onto the lawn, I could not resist and took myself and the baby outside. So I was standing there when I saw them, the baby in my arms: three tiny funnels that licked down from the cloud, tasting the red sky once, twice. They were so diminutive that I almost laughed. They looked like toy tops, whirling fast enough to appear still. I watched as they stepped delicately onto the thin horizon line and gripped it like tightrope walkers, whirring from side to side, but never stepping off the wire and now not so small. The dervishes glissed left and right, graceful and loose at the hip, steady above as though clothes-pinned at the shoulders to the line of cloud. The hailstones were coming faster and harder, but with my arm over my head and the baby's warm head tucked under my chin, I was able to avoid most of the stones by weaving a little as I hurried back toward the house. But our progress was suddenly arrested. There was a roaring inhalation, a great gasp from the sky, and the smell of ozone, shot in a blast straight to the back of my head, making me giddy. I let out an involuntary whoop, part laughter, part praise, and the baby must have felt it: she jack-knifed herself toward the air, using my chest as a platform. Her strong lungs filled and her sharp toes dug into my chest, and I held on. Her mouth and eyes flew open wide, and she waved her arms. I raised her up to see the tightrope dancers, the three spinning tops, both of us laughing now, gulping lung-fuls of sweet ozone as the barometric pressure crashed. I waved the baby; the baby waved herself. I laughed again and raised her higher, as high as I could.

I'm not sure what made me look at that exact moment, but I turned toward the house just in time to see my sister do a sort of cannonball off the steps of her porch. She cleared the three stone steps with ease, made a perfect two-point landing, and got her stride as she sprinted toward us across the enormous lawn. The noise of wind and hail was very loud, so I could not hear what she was saying, but I could guess: her mouth was shaped in fury, teeth biting her lower lip to get enough power into the squeezed, hissed *eff* sound of "you *flake!*" or "you *freak!*" or something familiar like that. Her face, contorted with effort as it was, was still noticeably beautiful. This is one of my sister's gifts: she has a pretty face, even in rage, and this has always been a distraction to me, and it was so, no less than any other time, as she gained ground. I was thinking of this, of how pretty she looked sprinting toward me and the baby, who I was holding up in the air. And maybe I was smiling a bit, thinking, *She's so pretty!* and maybe I said, "Pretty!" as my sister got closer, the *eff* sound clutched in her teeth like a bit. She lunged upward and grabbed the baby, still running.

Standing there with my arms stretched above my head, I was struck with an immediate, profound, and irrelevant understanding of football. I had heard an audible *snatch!* as my sister plucked the baby from my grip, and for a moment I saw the word suspended in a cartoon bubble over my head, right where the baby had been.

"Get in the car, you *fool!* You *ff*—*!* You *fuh*—*!*" she huffed, still running. "Get in!" she spat over her shoulder, reaching the car. She buckled the baby into her car seat in the back. "Just get *in*," she shouted and threw a bag of diapers through the open door. I followed the diapers, mute.

My sister gunned the engine, banged the car into reverse, threw her right arm across the back of the seat, and opened her mouth, but her words were lost in a sudden burst of rain that hit the car roof as though dumped from a big tin laundry tub upended after the wash.

We sped away from the house and the boiling horizon, me twisted backward to watch as the three little funnels spun and struck against each other, striking dust sparks from the bare one-acre plots. The three dancing tops drew together in an irresistible embrace, clasping their arms around each other's shoulders, heads bent beneath the black cloud cap, where they fused into one. It was the biggest twister my sister or I had seen, though we had both made our father stop the truck more than once to watch as a dust devil danced itself to extinction across some fallow field. He'd held the prairie farmer's superstition that you could always drive away from a twister at right angles, so my sister tried, cutting across subdivision streets and then grid roads, travelling north, then west. But this was taking us closer and closer to the city, and so we made our way south to the Yellow Head, the black witch on the horizon chasing us all the way.

In a truck-stop motel room west of Edmonton, we watched the tornado's progress on television, the three of us safe in a double bed. The baby seemed quite happy. I had put her in the big bed wrapped in my camisole, a good silk one. While my sister talked to her husband on the bedside phone, assuring him with her familiar mix of kindness and irritability that we were all well, I tied the bottom of the camisole into a knot, making a kind of baby bag. I tucked the baby in close to my side. She really did look like a princess, with her dark curls like fine smoke.

I lay in the big bed with the baby and my sister, watching the television with the sound turned off. I watched the tornado that chewed up Edmonton, devouring twenty-seven people and feasting on an entire trailer park north of the city. My sister fell straight down into a catless sleep, so I turned the television off. We lay there in a row, our heads of dark hair in a line across the pillows.

I flew back East a few days later. For several reasons, none of which I know, I didn't go home again for almost eleven years. I wish the tornado had picked up the house and dropped it on my sister. Our father had been dead a year when we saw each other that hot summer, and neither of us ever mentioned it. Not once. I keep trying to find the ending for that waking dream, but the closest I ever get is the sight of that big tornado. Sometimes it is in the black hand of the fairy as she draws it out of her sky-coloured bag.

Halo and Epiphany

The window blind breathes out and in once against the window, and the blades of the fan begin to move, so you know there is a breeze although you do not feel it yet as you lie smooth and emptied between the sheets. Your legs and hers beneath the sheet rustle lazily, sounding like tall grass in the wind. You hear the little song of the bird that foretells rain, and so you know the breeze and you know it is a cool one. It's the kind of breeze that comes first to say that rain will be along later.

You remember other times that you heard rain birds, when they were meadowlarks on the prairie, with their groundling nests hidden in the tall grass. The poplars smell magnificent and clean: a thin, high, light scent that says Hurry! The sky is perfect perfect perfect.

It is the summer between high school and university.

In the summer between high school and university, I went camping with two childhood friends. I had been best friends with these two girls, Michelle and Colleen, all through elementary school at St. Matthew's, but when it was time for high school they went to Sacred Heart, the all-girls school, and I went to the one run by the Brothers of the Society of Jesus. The Jesuits had just opened their doors to girls in 1976, the year I started.

For four years, Michelle and Colleen and I didn't see each other much. But I could see that over at Sacred Heart, something was happening to Michelle. She was becoming very, very beautiful, except for her face, and she had the biggest hair I had ever seen. She carried her head very carefully because of it, as though it were a nest full of blown-hollow Easter eggs. She looked almost exactly like a model, and her father was very proud of her and was always telling her to try modelling before she went on to university.

Colleen had stayed about the same during high school, as had I. I had rekindled the friendship with Michelle and Colleen by going to their graduation. Crashing it, really, with two guy friends. What stays with me—in relief sharp as a young girl's body silhouetted to the slip beneath her dress by the sunlight that blazes in through the open gymnasium doors behind her—what stays with me is the look on the faces of the mothers of Colleen and Michelle when they saw me there. It was a revelation that adults would openly hate someone my age. They had their heads tipped toward each other, not bothering to pretend not to stare, mouths moving fast and small. Eyes on me, lips pulled cornerwise in confidence, agreeing fast and long. One nodding, one talking.

I pretended that it was not happening. Rather, something inside me, a little switch, perhaps, simply clicked to off, and a small darkness descended over whatever feeling those eyes had ignited.

A few weeks later, I was allowed to pick up Michelle and Colleen in my dad's car, with a pop-up tent trailer, and take them camping. I think they were allowed because I was going to be there to change flat tires, chop wood, start fires, chase off bears.

However it came about, I was in charge, and I liked the feeling. When I picked up Michelle and Colleen in the Ford Galaxy, I avoided the eyes of their mothers. In front of Michelle's house, ready to leave for the lake, I idled the engine while Michelle's dad said goodbye to her. It gave me the creeps to hear him tell her how beautiful she was and to see him smile at her and hug her, carefully, so as not to crush her hair. Both Michelle and Colleen got in the backseat. I laid a little bit of rubber as I pulled out, not sure if I liked being chauffeur.

When we got to the lake, the leaves of the poplar trees were turning their silver backs out, the rain birds were chicking, and the sky was darkening. I said it was going to rain. We set up the tent trailer, getting ready to cook inside on the little propane stove, but when I started fiddling with it to light it, Michelle hissed, "*My hair.*"

"Hairspray," she explained. "It's flammable."

Michelle was tall and slim and straight and even. She wore short white shorts and a white tube top. She really did look like a model, but she also looked at that moment a lot like an oversized aerosol spray can, and my mind leapt to that little picture on hairspray cans that shows it exploding near open flame. I turned off the propane and said, "I'll make a fire."

Outside, in the odd stillness that comes before rain on the prairie, when the incessant wind ceases and you notice how busy the insects and the birds keep so their chirring is seamless, I got a little fire going, and we ate our dinner the minute it was hot. Michelle put a folded towel under her butt to keep her white shorts clean. Colleen and I sat on the ground. After a while I produced a six-pack from the trunk of the car. If there had been any boys around we would have pretended to be drunker than we were, but there were no boys, so we just sipped our beers out of the bottles until they were too warm to finish. The rain never came, and when the clouds tore up and drifted away, the stars came out.

I built the fire up. We put marshmallows on sticks and stuck them close to the flames. I acted tough a lot, and we laughed a lot, but I don't remember what we laughed about. Maybe it was just being together again after four high-school years apart. But we had been small together, and it seemed, while we were laughing at who knows what and drinking warm beer and feeling very grown up to be out camping alone, that no time had passed between grade school and then. We talked about what we were going to do in the fall. We were all going to university, Campion College, a Catholic college, named for Edmund Campion, the sixteenth-century English Jesuit martyr who had his guts drawn out, cooked over a little fire, and fed to him on the end of a pointed stick.

We talked about majors and electives and said *prof* and *professor*. We talked about guys and about clothes and guys even more, and then Michelle started saying that her dad was really encouraging her to model instead of going to university right away, and I started thinking, *Isn't anyone going to say anything about the fact that you can't have an overbite and beady eyes and bad skin and a nose like a guinea pig's if you're going to be a model, no matter how long your legs are or how big your hair is?* Michelle whipped out a hairbrush and started brushing her hair in the light of the campfire, and when my marshmallow caught on fire, and I started waving it around to put it out, I actually had a vision of the flaming marshmallow sticking in her hair and lighting it on fire before it happened, and then it did.

It went up like God in a bush. It made a woofing sound, and Michelle hooted then screamed then jumped up and waved her hands around her head, which did nothing, and then Colleen, screaming *yaaaah, yaaaah*, flung a beach towel over Michelle's head.

The fire was out. It was all over very quickly. So quickly, in fact, that when the screaming was done and Michelle and Colleen were clutching each other and crying—Michelle's head shrouded in a towel and Colleen hugging it to her chest like a flotation device—I was still laughing. It was very hard to explain that I was truly sorry and that it truly had been an accident and that I wasn't laughing because it was funny.

I couldn't say it, but I was laughing because though it really and truly had been an accident, I knew in the moment I saw my arm waving itself, holding the stick on which the marshmallow was burning and drifting toward the bush of Michelle's hair, I could have stopped it, if I hadn't, at that exact moment, had an epiphany that whatever happened was the divine will of God and that it would have been a sin to interfere with God's plan. I felt part of something larger, inevitable, brutal.

Michelle's hair was singed down in clumps like sticky nests on the right side of her head. Her scalp wasn't burned at all. I think all the hairspray made the hair go up so quickly that she couldn't possibly have sustained any injury, which was lucky.

I don't remember much else about the camping trip. It must have been a bit strained after that, and I think we headed back home earlier than planned. Michelle and Colleen and I did all go to Campion College in the fall, but I saw even less of them than I had during high school. I deviled the Brothers of the Society of Jesus over points of theology I had no real grasp of, seizing gleefully upon a deliberate misreading of *The Confessions* to argue that Jesus and Lucifer, the Lightbringer, the Morningstar, were brothers, or at least half-brothers, sharing one half of Divine Parentage. I insisted the will of Satan must be the will of God, or God is neither omniscient nor omnipotent. Campion College is not a big place, and the Brothers warned of what would happen if I did not rein it in. I didn't rein it in, and I was expelled from the college, and I suppose it served me right. Michelle was something of a phenomenon on campus, boys following her everywhere, Colleen nearby at a safe distance. In the fall of what should have been my second year, I dropped out of university entirely and moved to Toronto.

About four years after that I ran into Colleen on the Spadina line. She had the same eyes: round and blue and lavishly fringed and always worried, worried, worried looking, even when she smiled.

Concerned Colleen. She was very pleased to see me: her forehead wrinkled, her eyebrows rose up and in to meet each other in the middle, and she smiled broadly. Her eyes actually twinkled. When I saw them twinkle, I was happy to see her too. She was employed by a Catholic missionary society (when I found out she was more devout than ever I relaxed—I'd probably been forgiven a long time ago), and she was only in Toronto for a couple of days before going to Central America.

I was pretty interested in Daniel Ortega and the possibility of the Sandinistas winning, but it turned out Colleen was going to do some diocesan work in Panama. So we just talked about people back home.

I asked about Michelle, and Colleen told me in a hushed voice that Michelle had suffered a terrible scandal. She had become engaged, or pre-engaged, to a boy at Campion, a boy named Michael. But there had been rumours that her fiancé had been caught in a compromising relationship with one of his male professors. It was only a rumour, probably, but the professor was, and

here Colleen's voice dropped even more, "A Gay. A homosexual."
And Michelle's fiancé had hanged himself.

"Isn't that tragic?" Colleen asked. "Isn't that tragic?"

"My God how awful," I said.

On the subway seat, Colleen and I were rocked back and forth a little as the subway rounded the curve into Union station. Colleen patted my back.

"That boy," I said.

"I know," she said. "Michelle was devastated."

"My God," I said again.

"My stop is the one after this," said Colleen, still patting. "Are you okay?"

I was still rocking.

I had seen the boy, and he had been a beautiful boy with hair like an angel. He had moved in a constellation of male students clustered around one particular professor, a man of intelligence and separateness. The boy, I remembered, seemed to burn with a light from within, in a way that I wouldn't understand until I moved into an apartment at Church and Wellesley in Toronto and saw boys so happy to be kissing each other in public that Church and Wellesley seemed the brightest place to be on a hot night in the summer.

"Suicide is a sin, of course," murmured Colleen, "but poor Michelle. Why did he give her a ring? She had an engagement ring."

Colleen got up as the train approached her stop. "Poor Michelle," she said, swaying with the motion of the train, holding the pole and watching the door, but keeping an eye and a hand on me, too. "Poor Michelle," she said again. "Remember her in your prayers."

I kept my head down.

I managed to get up to hug her. A quick goodbye, me patting her now, a hand on her back as I thought: *one of us has become a Catholic missionary, and one of us has become a martyr to a suicide, an invert suicide, who betrayed a girl by being gay, and one of us will tell about it.*

At home in Saskatchewan, I had only ever seen that boy at a distance, but now, I saw him everywhere: in a crowd or going around the corner just ahead of me. My arm would raise itself in the air, and a shout would rise from my chest like laughter, but no sound ever came.

You could never shake the feeling that you were somehow a criminal after that. When fire was in the girl's hair it had looked to you like a halo. Whether it was hers or not, you're not sure. You think now, perhaps, it was the boy's, maybe, or maybe your own. It doesn't matter. It's gone out. As though that were all of heaven you'd ever get.

O Once in Her Life Tell Your Mother She's Beautiful

My friend Tanya calls me and tells me that she's read my story, the one I gave her to read, and that, furthermore, she has called her mother on the West Coast, in spite of the time difference. It's ten in Peterborough, so only seven in Victoria, but since Tanya has been up since early with Phoebe, whom she is trying to wean, at least in the night, she calls her mom and reads her the story over the phone. The whole story, right out of *Descant*, where it is printed.

She says to her mom, "I think you are going to cry when you hear this," and her mom says, "That's all right, baby, I'll listen, I'll listen," and doesn't bother to say, "It's seven o'clock in the morning."

So Tanya reads her the story, and her mother cries. She cries, remembering her own mother, dead of the same thing, and she thinks of her mother-in-law and about her own breast, altered now where she touches it, alive. She has been thinking about this a lot lately, what with Tanya and Tanya's baby, Phoebe. In fact, she was thinking about it when the phone rang. So she was awake, and it was no trouble to say, "That's all right, baby, I'll listen."

How many times in her own short life as a mother—fewer than a thousand days since Phoebe was born—has Tanya managed to get it right? Maybe once or twice. Once, she talked Phoebe's hurt away in a flood of words, a full-court press of correction and acceptance of culpability, of apology, insisting that she had been wrong and Phoebe had been right, and in the talking, the non-stopness of it, she watched the child's rage dissolve with her

183

tears, and then, to her surprise, something invisible flew away from the child, and Tanya did not know until it left that what had left was shame.

She has spent the first forty years of her life being not a mother, being a not mother, and you're thinking now, *What's this? Is this about motherhood, or not?* Or maybe you're not thinking about it, managing to not go to the visual on a forty-year-old first-time mother, because what does an old mom look like anyway? Does she look like an old woman? Tanya has grey hair. Everywhere. Even down there. She doesn't exactly look like a grandma, but she has lines on her face and her jawline's a little loose, and after nursing a baby, her breasts are different.

But what does it matter? The guy she thought would be her forever boyfriend is now the guy she calculatingly sized up a few days after the baby was born, deciding that if a scrawny-shanked she-wolf can take down a caribou armoured with club-headed antlers and running hooves and three times the wolf's weight—if a very hungry wolf with four or seven pups in her den will attack and kill a creature of this size, that is running in a herd of maybe thousands like itself, if a wolf-bitch will kill this creature with her mouth, with her teeth, with her face, then she, Tanya, knows that the minute the boyfriend looks the wrong way at the baby, if he thinks for a moment it's been a long, cold winter and he might have to eat that baby, then she knows that she too can kill him without a second's hesitation and with no weapon but her teeth.

But what does it matter? Louis Simpson said of Anne Sexton's poem "Menstruation at Forty" that it was "the straw that broke this camel's back," and there go all those straw women, lady writers, poetesses, scribbling away with their leaky bodies and wanting to tell you all about it, for God's sake, as if they neither have nor want privacy.

But that's absolutely not what this is about. It's not about babies or weaning or placentas or surprise C-sections in the night after twenty-four hours of incompetent contractions. Nor is it about nursing all night, night after night, until the morning, while running the vacuum around Lego pieces and having it dawn on you that the way to get soldiers, young men, boys, really, who were once that baby gripping your breast with a mouth that would forever after try to duplicate the intimacy of that kiss, would try to improve upon it, actually, in seeking a mouth that kisses back—that soldier was once a baby whose miniature scythe-edged fingertips pinchfisted your breast, rhythmically pressing it as though playing a concertina—and remember, they said the average age of soldiers killed in Vietnam was nineteen—nineteen!—the way to get young boys to kill each other or to follow orders into My Lai and then cut the tiny ears off the heads they have just sowed with bullets as though cleverly solving the problem of how to break open a watermelon for the pool party without the aid of a sharp knife—the way to get them to do that and then grin for the camera while holding up what at first glance appears to be walnuts is to first and foremost deprive them of sleep.

Torture has always included sleep deprivation: the solitary confinement cell with the light bulb perpetually burning, cold, heat, hunger, noise. Tanya thinks of the speakers aimed at the Vatican mission in Panama City that blasted "Dancing Queen" until Noriega ran out screaming, surrendering, hating ABBA for the rest of his life.

Tanya's mom sits up in bed, and her skin feels pleasantly dry. She powdered her legs with something expensive after showering and shaving them the night before, and as she slides them over the edge of the mattress, she inhales the scent with great satisfaction. Her daughter has called her in the early morning to read her a story over the phone about a mother and her daughter, and she is alive to take the call and say, "I'll listen, I'll listen."

But listen. Her name is Pamela, and she was already awake when Tanya called. She had been awake, thinking. So when Tanya is finished reading to her over the phone, and when they have both cried and stopped and said goodbye, she gets up out of bed, smelling the smell of her expensive body talc, and sits at the writing desk and writes a poem.

Now Tanya's mother is not my mother, and I don't really know if any of this is true, except that I wrote the story about the little girl and the bird in the clearing, and that I gave it to Tanya to read, and that Tanya's mother wrote a poem after she'd heard the story over the phone, after lying awake thinking of her mother.

But who's your mother, anyway? Who's writing her story and who's writing your story? Out of them all—Tanya, Tanya's mother, Pamela, her mother-in-law, Phoebe, me, maybe you—out of all of us, I am the only one untouched by that cancer of the body that strikes where love begins. Once in her life, tell your mother she's beautiful, even if you have to lie, even if she dreams of the massacre of innocents, even if she's so mean you want to fall down and die. Tell her she's beautiful. It's not the same as love.

I don't know what comes next in the story, so I take my own advice and I call my mother. I ease into it, telling her about a memory of when I had stayed at my aunt's, on the farm—maybe

186

two nights, definitely no more—and I was lonely for her the next day, and so my auntie said, "Come hang the sheets out with me," and so we did, beside the creek, down a little hill by the house which hid the road and driveway from view. She clothespinned wet bed sheets to the line and then went to milk the little Jersey cow, and I heard my parents' car pull into the lane.

For some reason I waited, crouched on one knee behind the sheets, until I heard my mother's voice ask, "Where's Janette?" then I came out from behind the sheets to watch my mom come over the hill, smiling and swinging her arms and in a hurry to see me—to see me!—and wearing a red Fortrel pantsuit and matching red lipstick, and she looked beautiful she looked beautiful she looked so beautiful I thought to myself *She's so beautiful,* and I was probably a little over seven years old.

I tell my mother this memory, and she makes this sound that is so characteristic of her and, it turns out, of me that I have heard my own little daughter make it. It is made by saying *hmmmm* skeptically, with a sudden stop and with the lips compressed. Technically, it is a snort since the final noise comes from the nose.

She makes this noise and says *Fortrel.* I am not going to take this bait. I am not going to get involved in what I know will devolve from trademarked names for polyester—but you must know that, for me, the Fortrel red of 1970 is still the Form of red against which all other reds are shadows in the cave—from some dismissive comment about the perfect red, the mother of all reds, to the questionability of pantsuits worn with matching lipstick, to how men are weak, to how my sister and I baby our husbands (which is not true), to how politicians are corrupt. If I take this cue, the conversation will end with her asking me some question which is unanswerable, such as "Who is there to vote for? Who? Those politicians. They're all alike. I ask you."

I stick to the agenda, and I say, "You looked so beautiful that I said to myself, 'She's beautiful.'" And then, for some reason, I add, "Maybe you looked so beautiful because I had missed you so much and was so happy to see you, even though I had only been away from home for maybe one night, two at the most. You know."

The *You know* referred to the fact that I simply could not be away from home overnight until I was about nineteen years old, I think. Not true. I could do it, and I did, by about age ten. But those ten-year-old sleepovers were insomniac and dreadful. I just wanted to be near Mama.

Now I tell my mother, "I saw a little girl once turn, crying, with her arms outstretched, toward the man who had just slapped her face. I stood by and did not move." I say to my mom, "What if we are like those flowers whose faces turn to follow the sun as it tracks across the sky? Heliotropes. What if we move toward love like sunflowers to sunlight, and we don't have any choice in it?"

Silence.

Well. We say goodbye. Make kiss noises into the phone. I am forty-one.

I remember gazing into the soundless, open, breathless throat of a deep red hollyhock bloom. For a moment I became miniscule, very quickly, with a sort of sipping sound, and entered the flower. I … what? I was about to say I grew large again, but none of this happened. I think, from my perspective now, that I had an egoless moment. I was very young and perhaps not so far removed that I could not readily retreat to the place where I had been, where we all were, where we all come from before we are born. Whatever arrangement of atoms made me separate from the flower was momentarily unmade, and I simply rejoined it as itself, before my self's speedy and complete reconstitution.

Tanya's mother rises from her writing desk. Once in her life, tell your mother she's beautiful. It's not the same as love. It's infinitely more terrifying and more real.

A continent's width away, Tanya's kitchen suddenly fills with the scent of bright and powdery perfumed talc. She thinks, *It's about connection.* It's about the connection between mothers and daughters no matter what. And she goes to find Phoebe.

Near Summerside, Pamela is standing in the empty front room of the house that looks out onto the ocean. The room is empty because she hasn't unpacked yet. They have just bought the house, just moved in, and Pamela has about two weeks before her due date. She will name the baby Tanya.

She is thinking of this, and of nothing, when a contraction forms, like a tiny wave rolling into itself off the coast in the deep, violent, secret, and menacing Atlantic trough. This is the first baby. Thoughts without words form in Pamela: Is this it? Can I stop it? These thoughts have no words, and to Pamela it is more like listening to a conversation between animals or stones. As the contraction breaks, Pamela discovers that whatever is happening is not about her at all.

A bird, graceless, slaps into the big, square picture window. Pamela puts her arms out, though safe behind glass, to protect herself and the pain she is in, and a white light fills the room. The white bird, in fact, fills the room, and Pamela is lifted up by its light, and what happens now is that she turns and sees one-year-old

Tanya toddling toward her down the bare hallway, and as she says *Tanya* she hangs up the telephone in a hotel room in Victoria.

Far away, Pamela rises from her writing desk. There is a difference between what is true and what is real. Any fool knows a story can be true without ever being real. Pamela is real, and Tanya is real, and I am real, and none of this is true.

Pamela feels beautiful, and she feels tall. Her body, to her, feels strong and curved like the stem of a lily. She knows she is magnificent. And she crosses to the window that looks out at the Pacific Ocean. She has lived most of her life facing the Atlantic from a stilted house that had withstood grief and bad weather. To her, the two oceans are distinct personalities: the Atlantic, deeper and narrower and darker than the Pacific she sees from her window, which is all that its name implies.

It is easy, then, to send herself out across the water, in the shape of a tern, to meet herself again more than halfway around the globe.

And is it true, then, even if it is not real, that she turns into a bird, that I turn this woman into a bird and send her flying into her own open arms?

Thirteen Ways of Looking at a River

A man stands on the riverbank, watching. Fair hair an incandescent white nimbus, insulating the skull within.

Electrical stimulation of the cortex during neurosurgery results in movement of the legs and arms. This was discovered by neurosurgeon Dr. Wilder Penfield, who mapped much of the human brain in the 1930s. In 1934, he probed an area of the right temporal lobe called the Sylvian fissure.

A woman wades into the river. At ankle depth, she leaves her shoes behind on the stony bottom. When the water reaches her knees, she lets go the hem of her dress. It makes a red pool in the water. The red pool moves with her. Her arms hang by her sides. When the waterline intersects her wrists, she stops. Another woman waits for her there.

Deep in the brain stem, insulated by the left and right temporal lobes, lies the bicameral system, a remnant from the Lower Paleolithic period, before the evolution of full human consciousness. Neuronal action in this part of the brain creates sensory phenomena that seem to originate externally, as though not generated by the subject. Bicameral activity presents as image, raw metaphor, not to be taken as fact.

In the river, the second woman reaches forward, drawing the blond head of the woman to her own. She kisses the woman in the red dress. The lips of the woman in the red dress are slack. She does not raise her hands. She does not step back. Her knees fold. She falls back in the water. The current takes her. The red dress billows around her as she is dragged downstream. The weight of the red dress is sufficient to sink her beneath the surface of the fast, clear water. She is pulled down the river in the pool of her red dress.

The bicameral system exhibits a high level of neuronal activity in the brains of artists and some other subject groups. Research on the bicameral area was begun on prison inmates in the 1960s but abandoned for humanitarian reasons by researchers citing increased stress levels.

To the woman in the red dress, the face of the woman in the middle of the river appears to be that of a wolf. The wolf face hovers translucently before and behind the real face that kissed, as when, without intermediary instruments, the bright disk of the sun is seen through cumulonimbus cloud. To the woman in the middle of the river, the woman in the red dress also has a face other than her own.

When the right temporal lobe is electrically stimulated close to the Sylvian fissure, subjects —wide awake and without pain, for the brain perceives pain from the body and has no ability to feel pain itself—report sensations of leaving the body, floating, hearing music, etc. The temporal lobes are part of the neocortex, which accounts for eighty percent of human brain mass.

The woman in the pool of red dress floats swiftly downriver. Her hair flows out behind her. It is a yellow stream in the clear river. Her memories flow out from the ends of her hair. Some catch on rocks. They are the hard green regrets of bad decisions. Some are trapped in eddies and whirlpools. They are longings for revenge. Others shoot into the air in a spray of white diamonds and disappear.

The right temporal lobe of the human brain is connected to the hippocampus, which serves as the master control, sorting out thousands of pieces of sensory input and deciding which of them should be acted upon. It contains unconscious desires and the ability to dream.

The woman in the middle of the river watches the woman in the red dress disappear. She licks her lips for the taste of their kiss. She is thirsty. She is patient. There will be another woman. And another woman after her. She has no memory, only thirst.

Surgical probing of the brain reveals that specific psychological experiences can be provoked by electrical stimulation. Specific areas in the limbic system, an ancient area of the brain located deep in the cortex, appear to be programmed for emotions of rage and anger.

The woman in the red dress rushes downstream. Fish swim behind her teeth like small tongues. The pool of her red dress and the yellow stream of her hair become part of the river. Cell walls lose their integrity. Molecules intersect, exchange information and structure. Hydrogen atoms bond, two to every atom of oxygen. Reintegrated, the red dress joins the river, a secret memory, an invisible stain.

Using planetariums that can project a changing night sky, ornithologists have demonstrated that birds raised in laboratories and never exposed to the night sky are born with a memory of the stars that enables them to navigate the inevitable migratory path. The cerebella of birds are proportionately enormous, relative to those of humans.

The woman in the middle of the river will stand there forever. Wait. Thirst. Wait.

The mourning warbler builds its nest in the flat swamplands of the Otonabee River valley, never far away from the view of poison ivy or deadly nightshade. Its migratory path takes it over the Niagara Peninsula and thence over Louisiana, Texas, and Mexico, until it reaches Ecuador, covering a distance of 2100 miles at night. The mourning warbler will not avoid any body of water that can be compassed in a single flight, including the 700 miles of the Gulf of Mexico. Some water birds making long voyages can rest on the waves if overtaken by storms, but for the luckless warbler whose feathers become water soaked, an ocean grave is inevitable.

On the day in 1991 when the man and the woman marry, parts of the body of the first victim are found in the water, encased in concrete.

His insistent caress draws me swimming up from sleep. I know this river, its wetness, its path. His body rocks mine. I let consciousness fly over us, a swallow carving purple arcs in the blue air above the river. Its flight brings it closer and closer to the surface of the water, but never below, where we swim together in the fierce current.

The first victim is a runaway, blond like her kidnappers, but not pretty enough. The second victim is dark, and lovely as a princess. Public outrage over the loss of the beautiful princess spurs the search for the murderers.

I offer him the thirst between my thighs. Drinking there, his eyes are green fishes in the river that I make of him. They swim toward the delta, dive, surface, dive again deeper. I arch silver over the water, intersecting the arc described by the wing tip of the swallow.

Everywhere, people help the search by wearing green ribbons. The helpful ribbons protrude from their chests like festive shrapnel, as though they had been caught in an explosion of gaily decorated bombs. Nevertheless, the second victim is found naked. When her body is lifted from its green ditch, it dangles surprisingly. The tendons of her ankles, wrists, and knees have been cut clean through.

On the river bottom, the stones are smooth and polished and brilliantly coloured, as though the stones were the eggs of birds with such extraordinary plumage that they could not be born.

My heart is a stone that will never stop sinking.

Some of This Is True

When we come out of the evening and into the Kinsmen Field House, people are mostly sitting in their seats. I drag Paula up front to the stage. I look back, and everyone is draining down the aisle toward us, like we're a bathtub plug that's just been pulled.

The hall goes black, then the lights come up on treble chops. Twelve.

There he is. Feet planted together, right leg jerking with each chop like he's trying to stomp change out of a hole in his pocket. Pointy-toed Docs, black jeans, pink socks. Cowboy shirt with the sleeves cut off, white star in a red circle on the t-shirt underneath.

When the bass line comes in, it rolls up like a hearse.

Paula thrusts her mouth to my ear and screams, "Oh my God I want to fuck him."

I'm thinking, "I want to be him."

I nail the first line, sing along so I'm part of the band. The war is declared and I nail it.

The girl I'm with, Paula, she got the tickets. She offered one to my cousin, who is an asshole. He didn't want it.

She's seen him pick me up after work. He flirts like it's involuntary: "Anything that squats to pee," he says, giggling like I'm going to agree with him.

Yesterday, Paula came into the tube room. We have summer jobs at the Sears catalogue warehouse in Regina. Mine is to stand in front of a rack of pneumatic tubes, flip open the dirty plastic canister that pops out, read the order, stuff the canister back up the tube, go fill the order, come back, and do it again. It's noisy, mindless, and pays more than minimum; it's mine because my mom used to work in customer service before she went on disability.

At the end of yesterday's shift, Paula followed me to the parking lot. She's tall, with a flat bum like she's on her back too much, and has really big breasts, so my cousin has his eyes on them when he says to me, "Get in back."

He looks at her shirtfront and turns the music up loud. When she leans in to shout, I see her mouth moving, but I can't hear her until my cousin punches the radio button. Then she's yelling, "—tomorrow night in Edmonton?"

Then, more normal, "Do you wanna go?"

My cousin frowns. "I don't do that punk shit."

"I'll go," I yelp from the back seat.

Paula looks confused but says, "Okay. We have to get the nine-thirty bus." She steps back from the car and does a fingertip wave.

My cousin turns the music up again and we pull onto Albert Street.

At home, he parks so close to the garage that I have to walk behind the car to get to the house. He's already opening his door and getting out, and he meets me behind the car. Grabbing my arms above the elbows, he says, "Gotcha!" like it's a game. He gets his face in close to mine and hisses, "What do you think you're up to?" He jerks his arms in around me and my feet leave the ground. My breath leaves my lungs in an ugly grunt. "Your fucking problem," he says, "is you're always trying to be different."

Drop.

"Don't even think of fucking going."

But I do.

Next morning, I go to my boss and say, "I've got to leave at nine for the doctor's."

"No way, José," my boss says, not raising his head. His scalp and hair are the same colour. "You know you change shifts twenty-four hours in advance. Besides," he says, looking at me over the top of his glasses, keeping his chins pressed into his neck, "Paula already used that excuse." He stares at my head for a long while, until I unclip my ID badge, put it on the counter and say, "All right. I quit." He frowns deeper in surprise.

By nine twenty, I'm in a Greyhound seat beside Paula. She has a mickey of Southern Comfort. She wants to talk about my cousin. The ride is ten and a half hours long.

"What's he like?"

"A jerk," I say. "Exactly like a jerk. He listens to shitty music and doesn't smoke dope."

"I like his car," she says.

"Uh huh." It's my mom's car, but I don't tell her.

"We went driving around last night," she offers, "after we dropped you off."

"Yeah?"

"Yeah. We went to Wascana Park and drank some beers and then we went back to your place." She giggles. "I gave him a blow job."

I already know this.

"Why'd you do that to your hair?" Paula says.

"I don't know. Felt like it."

"Your cousin is cool," she says.

I say, "He doesn't like punk."

"Neither do I," she says.

"Why'd you buy tickets?" I ask.

"I didn't." My heart skips a beat. "I stole them from my sister. She's going to shit."

I hate this girl. I feel sorry for her sister. But I'm glad I'm going.

"So, let's get drunk!" she says.

"No thanks," I say, turning my face into the seat, shutting my eyes.

The bass line rolls up the tail end of the song, and a rooster crows.

Last night, after my cousin and Paula dropped me off, I sat on a kitchen chair beside my mom's bed in the living room. The hospital bed didn't leave room for a couch. I turned her onto her side, made sure her arm wasn't stuck underneath. I watched *Love Boat*, put Vaseline on her lips. I ate some soup then watched *MASH*, holding her hand. She didn't wake up, or come to or whatever it's called, when I kissed her forehead and checked her IV. We call it the living room even though she's dying in it.

A guitar string hammers Morse code short short short long long long short short short—just like on the record. Ess oh ess. Ess oh ess.

My mom's hair never did grow back in. When she was allowed to come home, nobody expected her to last more than a few weeks. My cousin was still working at his job when he moved in to help out.

I hold my mom's hand, listen to her breathing and mine, and think, "What a knob. It's not about going. It's about coming back."

Darkness. Then the spy-movie guitar riff, and a single spotlight picks him out. He grabs the neck of his guitar, peels it off over his head. He raises it high and, without looking, hurls it straight-armed into the dark behind him. He grabs the mike, growls, "Driiiiiiive." Boomboom. "Drive." Boomboom.

When I hear my cousin come in the back door, I turn the TV up. Even so, I can hear his voice, and then a laugh in reply. After a while, I go down the dark hallway toward the bathroom. I have to pass my cousin's room. The door is open. They're not in there.

I walk down the hallway. The light from the TV in the living room flickers on the walls so that it's all underwater blue. Everything feels slow as I get closer to my room. The door is open and what I see first is Paula's dirty foot soles. Her toes are curled under, and she rocks slightly on her knees. Her bum is covered by her skirt, but she has no shirt on. She's got her arms on the bed, hands in fists, and he's holding her head down.

My cousin's eyes are aimed at me so I stop and figure out too late that he isn't seeing me. Then he is.

The Kinsmen House is full of screaming but everyone shuts up when Joe Strummer knee-drops to the stage. He falls forward and grinds the side of his face into the floor, holding the mike down. He tells it: "Baby, baby, won't you hear my plea." He says it again, like a hiccup, like a sob. Everyone starts screaming again.

Beside me, Paula bawls to nobody in particular. "I wanna fuck him! I wanna fuck him!"

"Why don't you just fuck everyone then, you fucking hose-bag!" I scream at her, hurting my throat. She opens and closes her mouth, all happy, like I've said something nice. She holds her fisted hands out, both thumbs up, waggles them like we're thinking the same thing. She hasn't heard me at all.

My cousin's eyes fasten onto me. He locks his elbows, ramming his hands into my old bedspread. He's pumping so fast that his chin points at me—you, you, you—with each thrust. I try to stop looking, try to make my feet move. I want to go back to my mom, but when my feet do start moving, they take me down the hall to the bathroom. I go in and lock the door, slide down with my back against it, onto the cold tile.

I sit there for a long time. I run a bath but don't get in it. I'm glad the TV is on loud.

After I figure they've gone, I open the door. The hallway is dark. It's quiet.

Back in the living room, I find out why: for some reason my asshole cousin has turned the TV off.

Also, my mom's not breathing.

Joe Strummer is on his hands and knees, circling the mike. He puts his mouth close so his lips are touching it. "Baby, baby won't you hear my plea?"

Her IV is still in place. For a long time I sit in the dark living room. Her face looks calm. I bolt the front door and the back door, hoping that bastard will stay out all night.

I get into my mom's bed with her, stay there all night.

In the morning, the house is cold. My mom is cold. Even though I know she can't feel it, I tuck the blankets in around her arms and legs. The bones, bone thin.

In the bathroom, I use scissors to get my hair short all over, then a safety razor on the sides to get down to the skin. It makes me look more like my mom.

He stays low on the stage. I can almost touch his Mohawk. His left arm is jack-knifed back, choking the mike stand. When he whips himself up to standing, the sweat from his face and hair splashes my fingertips.

He leaps for the mike. "She ain't coming back!"

Squeezed upright beside me, Paula is danced up and down by the press of the crowd.

"She ain't never coming back!"

I am happy. I wish I could raise myself up higher so Joe could see my Brigade Rosse shirt. I bob my head so hard it hurts my neck.

I know I am not Joe Strummer. He is the frontman of the only band that matters, and I am a teenage girl from Saskatchewan.

The stage edge cuts under my arms as I reach. The drummer counts it in, "One-two-three-four!" Drums and bass crash into each other. Feedback slices like a bullwhip overhead, lasts as long as the sting of a whip might. The drummer plays like he's sprinting on the spot.

Joe Strummer turns his head to listen to something, mouths, "What the fuck?" Nods at what he hears—was it *Cincinnati?*—then nods at the bass player, who is all long legs, leather, and biceps.

The pressure of the crowd is too much. I push back, use my elbows.

Instead of more room, I suddenly have less. I am vised between bodies that piston up and down, squeezing me off the ground. Paula is five or six people away. I reach my hand to her. She's yelling straight up into the air. My breath is pressed from me. My arms are on the stage, but my vision is going funny.

"Hey, hey," cries Joe, then, clang buzz scrack. The music grinds to a halt. "Fucking bedlam, innit? Shut it off."

I think the music has stopped, but I could be going unconscious or into a dying dream, because Joe Strummer and a roadie each have one of my arms. They are scraping me over the edge of the stage, my ribs a xylophone. My studded belt catches on the stage edge, and for a second I am stuck. Scrape of metal fly, kneecaps, shins. Then over, and I am beached on stage.

I try to stumble up, get my feet and knees under me. A hand is on my arm. I reach up.

I have hold of Joe Strummer's forearm. He looks right into my eyes. Doesn't smile, just looks.

His eyes are narrowed. His mouth is opened slightly, jaw relaxed. I can see the tip of his tongue.

He's busy, that's all. Saving people, I think.

Then he smiles, showing shark teeth.

The drummer counts in "Clampdown" again. The ones who have been hauled to safety onto the stage, stranded punks like me, start to dance, heads banging, washed by feedback.

Joe Strummer smiles maybe at the white star on my red shirt, maybe at my straight leg jeans, at my hair, I don't know what. He pulls me to standing, puts one hand on either side of my head, where the skin is still smooth from last night, draws my head toward his, ducks so that his forehead touches mine, resting together, keeps his hands on the sides of my head and shrugs his shoulders so I know to put my hands up, too. I wonder what it must look like from the audience, what we look like with our foreheads together and our Mohawks touching. The subsonic growl rhyme that should come next in the song doesn't because Joe Strummer is whispering instead, whispering and whispering to me only, so that his breath dries the sweat from our skin. He rolls his forehead against mine and whispers and breathes, and what he says is so low that I already know it will take me years to figure it out. For a moment, he lets his cheek rest in my open palm.

Then everything drops out.

Kick snare kick snare kick snare kick snare kick snare kick snare kick snare kick.

Joe's hands let go, and he lunges to the mike: "What are ya gonna do now?"

I let my lungs fill with air, and it feels like the first breath I've drawn in twenty-four hours. So I draw another breath. And another. And another.

Very Star

In the navy sky the pursed lips of the yellow moon whistle-flap in snorey rhythms that blow the tassel end of its long night cap up and down to reveal-conceal one sleeping eye, shut, long lashed and flat. A star squeezes out from the pointed moon's crescent chin with the sound of a cork popping. It drags behind it letters that spell *pop!* in jagged outlines, and a fast-moving fishing line follows. The sky expands with the sound of a slide whistle, and white stars prick through: *plink*, *plink*, high grace notes on a toy piano. The star drags the line as it drops through the sky, past planets, starlets, rockets that spin, through clouds, over rooftops, chimneys, steeples, smokestacks, train tracks, bridges, quilty fields of fence-trimmed squares, treetops. The star drops fast and heavy, pulling the line like spider gut silk. It punctures imperceptibly the slanted rooftop—brief silence as it falls soundlessly through the attic's emptiness, soft *pffft* of plaster and paint.

The star is studded with many points, like a swinging mace or meteor, and stops with a muffled thump. The soft hair it lands in puffs and settles, a brief cloud. The star has missed the skull, and so anchors adjacent in the percale and feathers of the pillow. There has been no meteoric impact; still, the child cries out without waking or words. In the next room, Mama and Papa hear the cry and freeze, hands up, fists tight, arms extended, fingers pointing, gown twisting, mouths working, trousers loose.

The child continues her dream in the unheard quiet that follows the unheard whisper-shouts that followed the tale of the nana who left the girl standing outside of the house, in the yard without a fence. The girl is four and Granddad is old or oblivious or foggy with Percocet so does not see while stumbling to midday beddy bed that his wife is gone with the baby and the child is waiting to hear who will watch me? Granddad lurches up the stairs to the house, fumbles the aluminum latch, and the pneumatic hiss is followed by a click as the door shuts behind him. In the grass, the girl holds her crouch, freezing movement to direct all senses to the answer that isn't coming. She bends over the figures in the grass: a bunny, a baby bunny, and another baby bunny, this one is the big sister bunny, and there's the daddy. Her breathing remains steady in the huff-puff rhythm of deep play, and she rocks slightly with the beat of her own heart, but her eyes move left and right in quickening alertness. Then she sees herself from the outside, in a great sea of green, the tended lawn of a suburban home unseparated from the tended lawn of a suburban home, unseparated from, et cetera. She sees a light bulb flash on in the air over her head, and her perspective swoops back down to rejoin her as she climbs the steps to the house, heads inside to the bathroom, flips the lock, shuts herself in safely to sit on the edge of the bath and cry quiet as a mouse until sobs become loud and then *Mama, Mama*. Percocet dreams are thick as night, and Granddad slumbers peaceful and innocent as any addict.

Nana rocks the babe off to Nod and goes to the kitchen and does not know how much time has passed. Funny story, says the nana to Mama later while Mama struggles to hold the happy, moving baby in one arm and the quiet, still girl by the hand. Girl was left outside by herself, don't know how, but he didn't know, found her locked in the bathroom and crying, ha, ha was not that silly.

From Mama's ears, lines flare out toward small clouds. The top of her head rises like a lid, and Mama's face gets red. The sound of a boiling-kettle-whistle scream. Nana smiles her best smile.

You should have come when I called you, girl says to Mama in car. I could not hear you. I was in the city. You should have come. I couldn't hear you. Then I should have called louder. Oh my darling, Mama is sorry. Mama loves you. Why was I so scared? asks the girl, still a little afraid. Are you crying, Mama? Yes, sweetie. Mama is in a rage, but Mama does not say this. Mama won't let that happen again. Here, let's have a song. The baby has fallen asleep in his car seat already and so doesn't sing along.

After bedtime there is a talk. Your mother, says the mama. You're kidding me, says Papa. I will never, says Mama. You must have heard wrong, they would never, are you sure? They are out of bed and cold-footed on the floor now, hands up, fists tight, arms extended, fingers pointing, gown twisting, mouths working, trousers loose. In the next room they hear the girl child cry out, wordless and without waking, and they freeze. They see each other in postures of rage and smile together, released from the game of frozen statue by their love for the child and each other. Together they go to the child's room, open the door a little to peer in. Light from the hall stabs a yellow shaft through the doorway, cutting across the wall and piercing the star-shaped nightlight above the child's head. Papa tiptoes across the blue carpet, turns on the starlight with a click, tiptoes back with the grin on his face that says to Mama, isn't this the very best thing. He joins her in the doorway, and they lean against each other's shoulders, gaze at the child. She's forgotten already, they say to each other in whisper voices. No harm done.

The girl kicks involuntarily in sleep, as a dog dream-runs, chasing its dream-prey. Hiding from Mama and Papa, the playing-dead star stirs, humps itself over the earlobe and into the ear canal. It humps, it rolls. It pierces the eardrum, the hammer, the anvil. The star draws the thread up, stitching the sky to the ceiling, the night to the bed, the story to the girl. It passes through the cortex, the limbic system, and the neocortex. The girl's scream arrives in the moment of waking, but there is no permanent suffering beyond grief. She clutches her ear, but no damage is done. Nothing is secreted. There is no sensory impairment the doctors can detect. Still, there are things the girl cannot hear, and there are things the girl can hear which are unheard by others.

Of course she grows up to become a dancer, and of course she dances the first female Petrouchka, the soulful marionette whose hopeless love for a doll leads to murder. Her Petrouchka is stellar: her leaps, hummingbird-like; her landings, absolute as crucifixion, anchor her feet to the stage.

The mama and papa are not surprised. They have always known there are things only the girl can hear. The granddad is oblivious. The nana is dead or happy. The baby, grown through the casual torture of childhood, burns with love and pride his whole life through, but rarely more brightly than when he watches his sister dance. He is a surgeon, whose skill in the operating room is matched only by his innovation: he designs and casts his own instruments—gold tips as tiny and delicate as the snout of the star-nosed mole, connecting through the cosmos with fibre-optic threads, mapping the constellations of the brain.

No harm done. This is your bedtime story this is your bedtime story good night good night good night.

About the Author

Janette Platana was born and raised in Saskatchewan and now lives in Small Town Ontario, where she writes, plays music, and makes short films. Her writing has been published in Canada, the United States, and Turkey. Of all places. She is grateful for the support of the Ontario Arts Council, the Canada Council, and the Chalmers Foundation.

Acknowledgements

Some of these stories have appeared in the following publications:

"Bloodline," "My Baptism," and "Thirteen Ways of Looking at a River," in *Descant* and *Paralelin Otesinde: The Turkish Anthology of Canadian Fiction.*

"Dear Dave Bidini" in *This Magazine* as the 2009 First Place Short Fiction Winner of The Great Canadian Literary Hunt.

An early version of "Easter" in *Kiss Machine.*

"Some of This Is True" in *Broken Pencil* and *Can't Lit: Fearless Fiction From Broken Pencil.*

"The Weather" in *dANDelion.*

Stories are written by a single author, but the people who make writing possible are almost infinite. My gratitude goes to Bill Shepherd, Nick Shepherd, and Rosalyn Platana. Thank you, Michael Caines, Kathy Kranias, and Michelle Berry. Thank you to Halli Villegas. Thank you, Deanna Janovski, for being a brilliant editor. And very special thanks to Kate Story, Ryan Kerr, and Joe Davies.